THE SPIRITSTONE SAGA

TARIQ
and the
TEMPLE OF
BEASTS

NEW YORK TIMES BESTSELLING AUTHOR
SARWAT CHADDA

ORCHARD

ORCHARD BOOKS

First published in Great Britain in 2024 by Hodder & Stoughton

1 3 5 7 9 10 8 6 4 2

A CIP catalogue record for this book
is available from the British Library.

ISBN 978 1 408 36930 2

Printed and bound in Great Britain by Clays Ltd, Elcograf S.p.A.

The paper and board used in this book
are made from wood from responsible sources.

Orchard Books
An imprint of
Hachette Children's Group
Part of Hodder & Stoughton Limited
Carmelite House
50 Victoria Embankment
London EC4Y 0DZ

The authorised representative in the EEA is Hachette Ireland, 8 Castlecourt Centre,
Castleknock Road, Castleknock, Dublin 15, D15 YF6A, Ireland

An Hachette UK Company
www.hachette.co.uk
www.hachettechildrens.co.uk

CHAPTER 1
TARIQ

Tariq shielded his eyes as he gazed across the sparkling sea towards the line of buildings appearing on the horizon. 'Our trip's coming to an end. Behold, New Ethrial!'

'Is that it?' said Artos, aghast. 'It's just a collection of hovels!'

'Nothing wrong with your eyes,' said Livia, lowering her telescope. 'Looks worse close up.'

'But it's my first command. Where are the

1

fortifications? There's no watch tower! No wall! How am I meant to protect it?' Artos complained.

Tariq shrugged. 'I guess that's part of your promotion? You couldn't be made a full knight of the Silver Guard and expect it all to be parades and dinner parties. You'll be fine, *Sir* Artos.'

'I'll be fine the moment I get off this ship,' muttered Artos, resting his forehead on the wooden rail. 'The sooner they build a bridge from one side of the ocean to the other, the better.'

Tariq pitied his friend. Artos was a born warrior, without fear and happy to take on an army by himself, but he quaked and turned pale – actually green – the moment he got on the water. It didn't matter if it was a rowboat or a ship like the Silver Mermaid, he suffered a lot and without respite.

Tariq had been born and raised on boats, but there had been some bad storms on the month-long crossing and even he'd felt wobbly at times, watching the waves rise to tower over their tough steamship.

Livia had loved it. Was it an elven trait to never get seasick or just her? She'd seen the whole trip as a jolly jaunt, spending as much time in the engine rooms with her instruments – taking measurements and recording outputs, whatever they were – as up on deck on clear nights, charting the stars. She looked glumly at the shore. 'Now what?'

Artos slowly raised his head and faced Tariq. 'Good question. That's a big jungle. You absolutely sure this isn't some wild goose chase?'

'It's here,' said Tariq.

'There's just an awful lot of "here",' said Livia, gesturing at the expanse of green. 'No one's mapped its full extent.'

Dandaka Jungle was the edge of their world. Beyond the small enclave of New Ethrial, where they'd be docking, was the vast unknown. But somewhere in that endless green was the Crocodile's Tear, the second of the fabled spiritstones: three magical stones that helped keep the world in balance.

The Crocodile's Tear had been given to the beast lords. The mortal races had been gifted the Heart's Desire and the elemental spirits had received the World's Egg. All three had been lost – stolen – centuries ago, thought lost forever.

Tariq smiled to himself. Not quite lost *forever*.

Tariq had been convinced they were only myths, until he and his new friends had tracked one down in New Ethrial, the World's Egg, and used it to stop a tidal wave from destroying the entire city.

But Livia wasn't wrong; there was an awful lot of 'here'. How would they find the Crocodile's Tear? He didn't even know where to begin. He'd hoped to get a stronger sense of it as they'd approached Dandaka, but there'd been nothing. That would have been too easy.

But wouldn't it be nice to have it 'too easy' every now and then?

Tariq pressed his hand against the satchel dangling from his shoulder. The World's Egg felt heavier than before. It had a strange presence, forever in the back of his mind. He'd sit on the deck, under the moonlight, watching the ever-changing colours glowing from within the fist-sized stone. He'd practise tapping into it, gently, and gradually using the spiritstone to connect to the elements around him. He would feel the immense power of the sea, the subtle pressures of the wind,

4

the furious energy of the furnaces in the heart of the ship, and the faint yet inescapable pull of the land beyond the horizon.

At first he would merely enjoy the sensation of becoming part of the ebb and flow of the elements, of their lurking power, but slowly he would use his connection to make subtle changes. He could raise and lower the wind, or alter the currents, even control the waves. Not by much, not often . . . *yet*.

The ship chugged along closer to the shore. Three sailing ships were anchored in the bay. New Ethrial's docks couldn't handle big ships yet but the construction of permanent stone quays was underway. Small fishing boats bobbed in the shallow water and seagulls circled overhead. The sun was intense on the arrivals' backs and dazzling as it reflected off the water.

The deck vibrated as the engines began shutting down and there was a satisfying splash as the anchor went overboard.

Artos sighed. 'I just want some solid ground under my feet.'

Livia pointed over her shoulder. 'We'll still have to go back home, sooner or later.'

'Ahoy there!'

All three peered over the railings.

A gilded rowboat bobbed alongside the steamship, with six oarsmen wearing heavily embroidered tunics. At the prow stood a platinum-haired elf waving his feather-festooned hat. 'Ahoy there! Do I have the honour of addressing the saviours of Ethrial? Surely you must be Tariq, Livia and . . . Sir Artos?'

'We are,' answered Livia. 'And who are you?'

The elf swept his hat in an extravagant bow. 'Lord Marius Silverbrow, governor of New Ethrial, at your service.'

'Lord Marius?' Artos said, suddenly rising from his misery. 'Didn't you once manage my father's vulcanite mines?'

'I am honoured that my minor service to your esteemed father left an impression! It was he who, very kindly, recommended me to this post.'

'The mines had never been more profitable,' said Artos.

The elf's eyes glinted. 'It's all about efficiency, Master Artos.'

Tariq's skin prickled. He'd heard the mines were worse than the prisons, with prisoners digging deep underground where cave-ins and collapses were common.

Lord Marius snapped his fingers at the rowers. 'Do make some space! And where are the cushions? How are these three heroes expected to travel unless there are cushions? We're not savages, you know!'

Artos swallowed. 'I . . . er, I'll wait until the captain's lowered one of the bigger rowboats.'

'Nonsense!' declared Marius. 'There's plenty of room! You'll do me the honour of staying at my mansion. It has plumbing!'

Livia nudged Artos. 'Can't get more civilised than indoor plumbing.'

There was nothing for it. The captain had a rope ladder slung over and agreed to have their luggage taken to the governor's house later. Livia went first, lightly landing on the rocking vessel and settling down on a velvet cushion beside Marius. She waved up at them. 'It's perfectly safe!'

Artos peered down the ladder and gulped. 'I'll go next. If I fall in, you will save me, won't you?' he asked Tariq.

Tariq frowned. 'In all that armour?'

Artos had wanted to make an impact. He was, after all, Sir Artos now, the youngest knight ever in the Silver Guard. His armour was made of the finest steel and extravagantly engraved, and Artos wore his silver sword proudly on his hip. Unlike the elegant longswords carried by the elves, his was a broad chopper, which he'd nicknamed Cleaver. But being dressed head to toe in metal was not ideal as swimwear.

Artos scowled then climbed down. He had to be grabbed by two of the rowers as one foot slipped off the edge of the rowboat, but he managed to scramble to his cushion beside Livia, clutching her hand as the boat bobbed.

Tariq joined them, perching up at the prow, feet dangling over the edge, gazing at the shore.

'Everyone comfortable?' asked Marius. Then he clapped his hands.

The rowers took up their oars. They looked

overheated and ridiculous, straining at the sea while dressed in thick tunics with stiff collars and tight belts. Lord Marius looked just as overdressed with his fine knee-high boots, tunic and massive hat, but there was more to him than a bad sense of fashion.

Lord Marius spread out his hands in an extravagant welcome. 'I am truly humbled to be hosting the saviours of Ethrial! I have, of course, heard all about how the three of you saved our city, the very jewel of the world, from catastrophe. They say the tidal wave was a hundred metres high and would have demolished the sea wall as if it were made of sand!' He turned his gaze sharply to Tariq. 'Yet you were able to reduce it to a mere ripple with your sorcery. To imagine, a seer visiting my humble half-built colony by the edge of the wilderness.'

Tariq blushed. He should have been used to the wild stories by now and how the tidal wave got higher with each telling. 'I had a lot of help, my lord.'

Lord Marius waved his hand dismissively. 'Help? To be sure. Livia, did you not win the

9

annual prize at the Guild of Artificers for your boat? What was it called?'

Livia grinned. 'The Seahorse. Yes, the annual prize and a promotion from apprentice to journeyperson. I'll be a fully qualified engineer in five years.'

Lord Marius shaded his eyes as he gazed back towards the ship. 'And where is your noble steed? I had hoped you would have come galloping over the waves on it.'

Now it was Livia's turn to blush. 'It, er, sank.'

Lord Marius sighed and there was a tear hanging artistically in the corner of his eye. 'I am bereft. But I understand you have brought your latest creation along? To assist in our work?'

'The Harvester,' said Livia. 'We'll be clearing the forest and building farms and houses in no time at all.'

Lord Marius clapped. 'Splendid! There is no stopping progress!'

Artos groaned as he leaned over the side of the rowboat.

Lord Marius patted him on the back. 'And last but by no means least the heroic Artos. I must confess I was . . . bemused that a korr would wish to join the Silver Guard, but now I have finally met you I realise that you are the perfect person to organise the defence of our small colony. What say you, Sir Artos?'

'Urgh,' said Artos.

'Quite right,' replied Lord Marius. 'Now's not the time to discuss such matters. Best saved till after you've seen the place.'

The rowboat struck the surf. The rowers leapt out and dragged the boat out of the water and on to the narrow beach.

The elven lord rose proudly and waved his hat.

'Ladies and gentlemen, welcome to New Ethrial!'

CHAPTER 2
LIVIA

'What's happening over there?' Livia pointed to a cluster of shacks on the outer edges of the town. Marius had been taking them up what he called the Grand Avenue – which was, in reality, a muddy half-paved track that led from the docks to the town – when her attention was caught by a row of shabbily dressed people busy chopping down trees and trimming off branches, stripping the trees down to logs. Equally ragged children were tossing scrub on to fires, smothering the shanty village with smoke.

Lord Marius covered his mouth with a dainty lace handkerchief. 'Just clearing more of the forest. Nothing to be concerned about.'

'Why are there guards?' she asked.

Not Silver Guards but brutish-looking thugs armed with clubs and short-barrelled fire-spitters patrolled the village, some with savage dogs straining at their leashes.

Lord Marius clearly didn't want to discuss this; instead he tried to lead them in the opposite direction. 'My mansion is this way. Don't you want to freshen up after your long journey?'

But Livia wasn't interested in Marius's gaudy over-the-top home. She headed towards the shacks.

Some workers were chained, with manacles round their ankles, so they had to shuffle while loaded down with sacks of soil or dragging branches for burning.

A dog barked and the guard jerked it back as it snapped at her. He wiped his sweaty face. 'This ain't the place for fine ladies, miss. Best you get back.'

'Who are these people?' Livia asked.

The guard grimaced as he turned towards the workers. 'Criminals. Every single one of them.'

'They've been shipped?'

Why hadn't she realised? It was the new punishment back home. At first only dangerous criminals were being sent to work in the colonies that were rising up at all points of the compass, to serve out their sentences digging, chopping, quarrying for the greater good, the greater profits, of Ethrial. But month by month the list of crimes punishable by shipping grew longer and pettier. Murder? You're shipped. Steal a loaf of bread? You're shipped.

Livia cast her gaze over the pitiful group. 'Why are some of them wearing chains? It's not as if there's anywhere for them to escape to.'

'It's punishment for troublemakers, miss.' He waved his fire-spitter towards a mud-splattered figure wrenching up a tree stump. 'Like her. She's one of the worst.'

Livia looked over at the prisoner in question. It couldn't be. Yet the more Livia stared, the more she realised it was. 'Foriz?'

14

By now Artos and Tariq had caught up. Artos glanced back towards Lord Marius. 'That was rude, Livia. You can't just wander off when—'

Livia pointed across the field. 'Recognise her?'

Artos frowned. 'Who? I don't know anyone . . . Oh. So *that's* what happened to her.'

They'd met Foriz back in Ethrial, when the young woman had been the rich and powerful head of a smuggling ring, a queen of crime. She'd offered her help in finding the World's Egg, only to betray the trio at the last moment and try to flee with it. Then the tidal wave had come. They'd only managed to get the Egg back because of Livia's boat the Seahorse.

Livia wasn't sure if she was angrier at having been betrayed or the sinking of her boat. Foriz had escaped in all the confusion, and Livia had thought they'd never see her again. Certainly not like this, her once thick red curls all shaved off, her skin covered in ground-in dirt and her lavishly embroidered outfits of silk and satin reduced to filthy sweat-soaked rags.

Foriz had spotted them. She stared, eyes narrowed with hate. Her body was thinner than

Livia remembered, yet there was defiance in the way she held up her head and the hardness of her gaze.

The guard chuckled. 'See what I mean? She looks like she'd bite out your throat. Tried to escape five times and she's only been here a month. On half-rations now. That'll break her spirit.'

'They all look like they're on half-rations,' said Livia. 'I thought there were laws regarding how prisoners were meant to be treated.'

The guard's good humour faded. 'Maybe in Ethrial, but we do things differently here. They're scum of the earth, miss. You can't expect to treat them like decent folk because they ain't decent folk.'

Tariq frowned. 'Some of these people are from the clans. Those there are mountain folk. What was their crime?'

The guard shrugged. 'Don't know. Don't care. All that matters is they chop and dig and everything's fine.'

Tariq narrowed his gaze. 'There's nothing fine about any of this.'

'I need to speak to Foriz,' said Livia.

But Artos shook his head. 'And say what? Foriz almost destroyed Ethrial with her greed! If you ask me, her being shipped is exactly what she deserved. Come on, Marius's waiting.'

'You go. I'll catch up. It's not like I can miss his house.' And before either of them could object she marched across the mud, even as the guard shouted at her to stop.

'Livia! There's no point!' yelled Artos.

Maybe he was right. She didn't even know what she was going to say, but it was too late – she was standing right in front of Foriz.

She looked worse close up. Her skin was covered with insect bites and swollen red with infection.

Livia pointed at the line of red bite marks along Foriz's arm. 'I, er, can get you something for that.'

'I'll survive,' said Foriz, not taking her eyes off her. 'What are you doing here? Did you cross the ocean just to gloat?'

'I didn't even know you were here,' Livia replied. 'I . . . assumed you'd escaped.'

'You didn't even . . . Never mind. Why don't you get lost? I've got to get this stump up or it's no food.'

'No food? All prisoners are entitled to be fed twice a day. It's the law.'

Foriz looped the rope round the stump, then across her shoulder. 'Take it up with Lord Marius. He makes the laws around here.'

Looking down at the tree stump, Livia could see the roots were in deep. There was no way Foriz would move it by herself.

'I've got a machine that'll do all that. It's why I'm here. To test the Harvester. It'll chop down a hundred trees in a day. In a month we'll have cleared all the forest around the town. We're making space for building farms, growing plenty of crops, plenty of room for grazing . . .'

Livia looked at the vast, endless jungle before her. No wonder everyone was so shattered. How could they hope to clear the jungle by hand? Each tree trunk was at least a metre thick!

'My machine will make things easier.'

Foriz laughed bitterly. 'Lovely. I'll be able to spend the rest of my days wiggling my toes in the river, fishing. A life of leisure, eh? I didn't realise I was out here for a holiday.'

'I'm trying to help you, Foriz.'

'No, you're not.' Foriz grunted as she took the strain. She was on her knees, trying to crawl through the mud. 'You're just trying to make yourself feel better. Now get lost before I get given another set of chains.'

'I'll go and speak with Lord Marius. We'll fix this.'

But Foriz didn't bother replying. She was locked in her struggle with the immovable stump.

Artos had gone with Lord Marius but Tariq had waited. 'What did she say?'

Livia scratched the back of her neck. She'd been bitten already and she'd only just got off the ship. 'They're being treated like slaves here, Tariq.'

He nodded. 'Then let's do something about it.'

CHAPTER 3
ARTOS

Artos clapped his hands as the servants brought in the food. 'Now that's more like it. I for one have had enough of fish stew and biscuits to last a lifetime!'

His belly rumbled as the smells flooded the courtyard, mingling with the scent of flowers and the musky odour of the nearby jungle. Crickets chirped from the branches as a servant lit the lanterns around the huge dining table. He helped himself to some chicken while knocking the table with his knuckles.

'Dandaka wood?'

Lord Marius waved his elegant long-fingered hand. 'Of course. Kilo for kilo more valuable than ivory, and here . . . the supply is endless.'

While Artos was entirely at home in these surroundings, Tariq was still shifting uneasily on his cushion. His river-clan friend had grown up eating cross-legged on the floor, the food spread across carpets woven from reeds. He never looked comfortable on a chair.

Lord Marius sipped from his goblet as he addressed Tariq. 'My reports from the Council tell me that you saved Ethrial from drowning with one of the spiritstones, the World's Egg. May I . . . may I see it?'

Tariq looked round at each of them. Artos knew he was reluctant to display the spiritstone because he was still learning how to use it. The World's Egg had helped save the city from the tidal wave, but it was a tidal wave the stone itself had actually *summoned*. It was dangerous in the wrong hands.

'All right,' said Tariq, reaching into his satchel, the one that never left his side. He took out the spiritstone and rested it on the table.

It was a crudely carved lump of rock slightly bigger than fist-sized and similar to marble. It was milky white and semi-transparent, but then colours hidden within began to shift, like trapped smoke, and the spiritstone glowed. A breeze swept across the courtyard, making the lanterns flicker and the trees above rustle gently.

Artos didn't have any magic in him at all, but even he could sense the unfathomable power of the World's Egg as it glowed more brightly, casting ever-shifting light across the courtyard. A red and yellow macaw perched on a balcony overlooking the space, cawed and took flight.

'Quite splendid,' said Lord Marius, captivated by the light. 'You can control the elements?'

Tariq put the spiritstone away and the magical moment ended. 'The less I use it, the better.'

Livia picked at the bread on her plate. She'd been in a grim mood ever since speaking to Foriz. 'You've built quite a place in such short time, m'lord.'

'The prisoners are a blessing,' said the elven noble as he helped himself to another goblet of wine.

'I doubt that's how they feel,' muttered Tariq.

Febian glared at him from across the table. 'They're criminals. They abused the society they were part of; it's only right they should make amends.'

Febian of the Silver Guard. Artos's heart had sunk when he'd found him waiting for them in the courtyard. One glance at the others and he knew they felt the same. How far did Artos need to go to get away from him? The elf warrior and he had had their problems, which included Artos punching him in the face. Artos smiled at the memory. Now that was a good day. For him.

Not so much Febian. Was it his imagination or was the elf's long nose not quite as straight as it had been? While most of the Silver Guard had grown to accept Artos into their elite ranks, not so Febian. He still believed that only elves should be in the Silver Guard and that Artos's presence somehow diminished it.

Livia's eyes narrowed as she met Febian's self-satisfied gaze. 'Some of the crimes are petty. One of the servants told me there's a woman who's been shipped here for stealing milk. Milk for her baby!'

'You shouldn't listen to servants' gossip,' said Lord Marius, his expression turning sullen.

Livia wasn't going to let this go. She leaned across the table. 'But is it true?'

'Crime is crime,' interrupted Febian. 'Artos agrees, don't you?'

Artos shifted uncomfortably as everyone turned their attention on him. 'People should follow the law. It's for their own good.'

'Is it?' snapped Livia. 'Or for the good of the coffers of those who run Ethrial?'

'My father always puts the interests of the city before his own,' replied Artos coldly. 'The capital is bursting at the seams, Livia. You know that, the Guild knows that. Out here? It's just wilderness that doesn't belong to anyone. Ours for the taking. Your machine will clear the forest. We'll have farms. Cheaper food for everyone. The Council's talking about free bread for the poor. Can you

24

imagine that? No one going hungry? Now tell me that isn't worth a little hardship.'

Livia scowled. 'Hardship for the prisoners, not us. We'll be building our success off the backs of people who are being treated like slaves!'

Artos chewed his lip. 'M'lord, there are laws on the treatment of prisoners.'

Lord Marius sighed. 'That is not something you need concern yourself with. Your job is to arrange the defence of New Ethrial.'

Febian helped himself to some grapes. 'We've had trouble. Nothing serious, but as the colony grows, becomes richer, it'll attract more criminal elements. The coast is already infested with smugglers and pirates. They attack the ships crossing the ocean then flee back to their strongholds hidden in the swamps along the coast. Then there are the beasts.'

'Beasts?' asked Tariq, suddenly attentive.

Febian's hand fell to his sword hilt. 'Wild animals that have no fear of us. The jungle's full of predators. More than one prisoner's been mauled to ribbons by a jaguar or dragged off by a hungry bear. A wall will keep the worst of them out, but we need to guard the river too. There's a crocodile.'

Lord Marius shivered. 'A great monster. Devoured an entire boat a few weeks ago. We've tried hunting it, but it's crafty.'

Tariq sat up, his interest piqued by the story. 'It been around here long?'

What was Tariq thinking? Artos wondered. They were here looking for the Crocodile's Tear and a giant crocodile was terrorising the small colony. Coincidence? Artos didn't understand the powers of the spiritstones, but legend said it had originally been gifted to the beast lords. Was the Crocodile's Tear influencing the animals of Dandaka? Or were the beasts merely defending their territory from invaders?

Febian stabbed at an orange with his eating knife. 'Sailors who've used this area are always boasting about monsters. But this particular beast is something special. Why so interested, Tariq?'

Lord Marius looked over at the river boy. 'Indeed. I know why Sir Artos and Livia have taken the arduous journey across the ocean, but not you. Whatever the reason, I am sure I can help.'

Artos looked over at his friend. 'I'm sure you can, m'lord Marius. But I wouldn't want to bother you until I am surer this . . . isn't a wild goose chase.'

Why hadn't Tariq trusted Lord Marius with the truth? But the river boy was a good judge of people. If he didn't want to talk about their quest, then neither would Artos. But there was business Lord Marius could help with.

'The wall's the priority, then we'll put up a tower to guard the river,' said Artos. 'But for that I will need workers who've been well fed and rested.' He reached into his tunic, pulled out a scroll and slid it towards the elven noble. 'Here's my plan. You'll see it's signed by all members of the Council.'

Marius picked it up, then turned pale as he read it. 'This is . . . ruinous. How can I afford all this? It'll eat into all my profits!'

Artos shrugged. 'It's for the good of Ethrial.'

Tariq chuckled, and as their eyes met, Artos winked.

Artos's father had pulled strings to get him this post. It wasn't fair, but Artos was beginning to understand that he could use his family connections to his advantage. They had needed to come out here, as Tariq was convinced this was where they'd find the Crocodile's Tear. Artos didn't understand how Tariq's powers worked, but he'd seen what the river boy could do. So he'd persuaded his father to arrange for him to come to New Ethrial to take charge of its defences. To build a wall, watch towers, arrange people to guard it. To protect the *investment*. His father understood that. But Artos needed workers, workers he'd be responsible for; workers he'd look after far better than Lord Marius.

Livia stood up slowly, pushing out her chair, the metal legs shrieking loudly on the flagstones, loud enough to make everyone grit their teeth. She yawned and stretched her arms. 'That was a lovely dinner. Now we're all very tired from a long trip and in need of bed. Aren't we? Say goodnight to our host.'

Artos stood up and performed a neat military bow. 'I look forward to us working together, m'lord. New Ethrial is sure to be a huge success.'

'A costly one,' muttered Lord Marius, responding to his bow with little more than a curt nod.

Tariq stretched as he stood, glad to be off that chair, and the three of them left the courtyard.

But the moment they were out of earshot of Lord Marius and Febian, Livia grabbed Artos's sleeve and pulled him round. 'And when were you going to tell me about your plans?'

'You've been too busy fussing over your machine. And this is my business, not yours.'

'And you know all about building, do you?'

'I may not be a member of the Guild of Artificers, but I know how to put up a fence. The watch-tower design is common throughout the kingdom, wherever the Silver Guard set up their bases. All I need is wood and a workforce. The workforce I get from Lord Marius, and you get me the wood using your Harvester.'

Livia fell silent.

He didn't like the way she was frowning. 'It does work, doesn't it?' Artos asked.

Livia polished her glasses even as she yawned. 'Back in Ethrial, yes. In case you hadn't noticed it's a lot hotter and wetter here. The humidity affects machines as much as it affects tempers.'

Tariq turned towards the main door leading out to the street. 'In which case I'm going to make the most of the cool night air. Go for a wander.'

'Stay within the town boundaries, Tariq. I mean it,' Artos warned. 'It's wild out there.'

'I grew up in the forest. I know how to look after myself.'

Artos shook his head. 'And that attitude is going to get you eaten by a tiger!'

CHAPTER 4
LIVIA

How could she help those poor prisoners? Livia was just a journey-person in the Guild of Artificers. She was here because she was good with a screwdriver.

The shipped were cheap labour. Lord Marius kept them fed just enough to work, desperate for their next meal but too exhausted to cause any trouble. It was inhumane.

Maybe Artos could turn things round, but she had a feeling Lord Marius wouldn't make things easy for the young knight. Febian certainly didn't want Artos to succeed. He and the governor would put a spanner in the works, maybe even the whole toolbox.

Livia didn't know what to do, but she had an idea. It was just like doing an exam: start with the easy questions first, the ones you know how to solve straight away. Save the big problems for the end.

She waited till it was late and left the mansion via the kitchen. By the time she came out she had two heavy sacks slung across her shoulders.

The streets were empty except for a few strays. Cats searched the refuse piles while dogs sat at doorways. One would glance up at her, flick away a buzzing fly with its ear, then settle down again. Livia wasn't any threat. The only sound disturbing the silence was the chorus of the cicadas.

She approached the edge of the clearing with the convicts' dwellings beyond. The guard she'd met earlier was snoring at his post. His big dog dropped the branch he'd been chewing and growled.

'C'mon, boy. You know me.' Livia tickled the guard dog's wobbly jowls.

They say elves have a way about them, a grace that the other mortals lack. It was the reason they made the best warriors; no one could handle a blade with the speed and precision of an elf. But it extended beyond that into all aspects of life. Elves had a natural talent for being at ease with whatever they were doing. Livia applied it in the workshop. She didn't work harder; she worked with less fuss and frustration. She'd seen how the other apprentices would get angry and dispirited, fighting against themselves. Elves didn't feel that, not much. Lady Fausta, her mentor, reckoned it was because the elves had an innate self-confidence. They accepted the way they were, and so did everyone, and everything, else.

Animals responded to her elven ease, which was why the guard dog just rolled over for her to tickle its belly.

'Oh, all right,' said Livia, giving it a good rub. The big brutish animal slobbered happily. Livia was just about to leave when she spotted the guard's fire-spitter lying in the mud. She tutted as she picked it up and inspected the fire mechanism. *That* needed a proper clean. If he wasn't careful it would blow up in his face.

She really should wake him and ask permission to take it, but then he'd ask what she was doing here and it would all get complicated. So she took out her notebook from Left-Hand-Side Pocket Four, scribbled her name and that she was staying at the mansion and tucked it into his pocket. Then she slung the weapon over her shoulder and walked on.

Foriz was exactly where Livia had left her earlier, slumped against the tree trunk. She hadn't even got back to her hut; she'd just collapsed where she'd stood. The young woman had her head under her arms, hiding herself away from the world as best she could. As Livia got close, she heard soft sobs and saw Foriz's chest shake.

'Foriz?' Livia whispered, embarrassed at witnessing Foriz so vulnerable.

Foriz jerked up, stared at Livia in pure horror and hurriedly wiped the tears from her face. 'What are you doing here? I told you to get lost!'

34

Livia clumsily dropped the sacks and pushed them over. 'I brought food in case you're hungry.'

Foriz eyed her suspiciously, as if this was some cruel trick, then ripped one open. She went in with both hands and pulled out a crusty loaf and a roast chicken. She tried to put both in her mouth simultaneously, refusing to risk losing even a moment between bites. 'Don't expect me to thank you,' she spluttered.

The stump hadn't budged a centimetre. She would need a draught horse to drag the roots from the earth. That or the Harvester.

Six blades and three pairs of claws, all powered by a double-chamber vulcanite engine. Lady Fausta's masterpiece. Livia had glowed with pride that she'd been chosen to test it, as Lady Fausta didn't travel well. Now she was a journey-person she was getting involved in the bigger projects, moving from the workshops to the laboratories where the real innovations were being made. Then one day she'd undertake a study of her own, and eventually promotion to Engineer.

But she had to get the Harvester working, out

in the heat and mud, and against trees a thousand years old with deep roots. If she failed, she might get demoted back down to apprentice, and there was no worse fate. She'd rather join the Silver Guard.

Livia wouldn't fail. She couldn't. The Harvester would be a triumph.

With the trees around New Ethrial all gone, the real building work could begin. No more flimsy buildings that would blow down in a strong wind. Neat streets with a parade of houses either side. A town square. Maybe with a fountain? She could design one in an afternoon.

Civilisation had arrived. Farms providing crops to Ethrial and beyond. No one hungry, anywhere. Now *that* was progress. An engineer's job was to make the world a better place. In a hundred years, not much time to an elf like her, there'd be a city here. She'd be able to tell her students that she'd helped build it when it was just a shanty town without a single paved street.

Foriz crunched the chicken bones between her back teeth and sucked each clean of the meat and marrow. She found the cake, tore off chunks and shoved them straight into her mouth, chugging down lemon water from the bottle Livia had smuggled out of the dining room. Crumbs, fat, grease and slivers of broken bone covered her tunic and her forearms. Foriz licked her fingers clean, carefully digging out the meat trapped under her nails. She burped loudly and turned her attention to the second bag, then stopped. 'I'll save the rest.' She looked back at the other prisoners sleeping nearby. 'They could do with some real food.'

'You're . . . helping them?' said Livia.

Foriz glared at her. 'And why not?'

'It's just, er . . .' Livia shook her head. 'It's just not what I expected from you. What happened?'

Foriz shook her manacles. 'This happened. I'm getting out of here, but I'm not going without—'

They both paused at the sound of a deep growl.

Foriz blushed. 'I can't help it if my stomach rumbles. It's still—'

'That wasn't your belly.' Livia stood up. The jungle beyond the town was a black void, but she sensed movement. 'It came from out there.'

37

A patch of silky shadow detached itself from the vast darkness of the jungle. Golden eyes shone in the moonlight.

A panther.

It was beautiful. And a little terrifying.

The moonlight glinted off its fangs as it snarled. Livia reminded herself elves had a way with animals, but looking at the beast she suddenly wasn't so sure it would roll over and let her rub its belly. She really wanted to run, but knew she'd never outpace the panther. She gulped and stayed very, *very* still.

It crept along the tree stumps, sniffing at a sleeping prisoner, its muscles sliding under its midnight fur. She'd read about the power of their jaws and the length of their claws. That had all seemed fine and fascinating in a book. Now, with it so close, she wished she hadn't read how utterly lethal such a beast was. She'd never seen a panther before. Did they all get so big?

'Get me out of these chains,' whispered Foriz. 'You must have a screwdriver tucked up your sleeve.'

'Just because I'm an artificer doesn't mean I always go out with a—'

'Do you have one or not?' Foriz snapped.

Livia huffed and pulled out her mini-tool kit from her pocket and flipped it open. It was a simple single-chamber lock. She needed the number four screwdriver and a file.

'It's getting closer,' whispered Foriz. It was heading straight towards them, padding silently through the stubble-strewn clearing.

Why wasn't the mechanism turning? Livia could feel something jammed in the keyhole. 'Did you try to open this yourself?'

'Maybe . . .'

Typical. Everyone thought engineering was just a case of bashing things with a spanner. Didn't they realise it was art? Better than art! It needed a delicate touch as well as a strong grip and a quick and slippery mind. You needed to know the rules, and when – and how – to break them. Livia wiggled the tip of the file into the keyhole. She needed to remove the wood that had broken off inside when Foriz had tried springing the lock herself.

'Livia. You need to hurry up.'

'It's . . . almost . . .' Just push, twist gently and . . . *click*. 'There. Done.'

The growl was at her shoulder. Her hair fluttered under the hot breath.

Livia looked round.

The panther snarled. Its whiskers brushed her cheeks.

'Er . . . nice kitty.'

Keep calm. There's nothing much else you can do, is there?

The big cat peeled back its lips, exposing its lethal flesh-tearing fangs. The golden eyes were huge, as if it was capturing every fearful bead of sweat on Livia's face. She saw her own terrified expression reflected in its hungry gaze.

It sniffed her. The growl rumbled deep within its chest.

'What's it doing?' said Foriz in a hushed voice.

Elves had . . . had a way with animals. Everyone knew that, Livia reminded herself.

Everyone but this panther.

It tilted its head, as if pondering. Then it puffed and sprang away. In moments it had cleared a dozen metres and leapt over a pile of logs and disappeared towards the town.

Livia couldn't put her tools back. Her hands were shaking too much.

'Let me do that,' said Foriz gently. She slipped the screwdriver and file away, then closed the tool kit and slid it into her pocket.

'That's mine,' said Livia.

'Oh.' Foriz handed it over. 'Old habits and all that. Now I can't say it's been fun, because it hasn't, but this is goodbye. Don't come looking for me.'

'Where are you going to go?'

'It's not your concern.' Foriz grabbed the second bag of food and slung it over her shoulder.

'You're heading into the jungle? How long do you think you'll last?'

Foriz kicked the stump. 'Longer than I would here.'

Livia couldn't argue with that. But there was more going on tonight than just freeing one person. 'That panther went into town. Wild animals don't usually do that, do they?'

'What do I care? Maybe it smelt your fine dinner.'

'People could get hurt.'

Foriz shrugged. 'Better them than me.'

'You don't mean that, Foriz.'

Foriz met her gaze, almost laughing. 'You don't know me at all, do you? If I were you, I'd get back on that ship and go straight home at first tide. The wilderness doesn't suit you, Livia. You're a city girl. All this fresh air? It'll be bad for your health.'

Why did Foriz make everything so hard?

They both jumped as an enormous roar shattered the silence.

After a moment's silence, the jungle replied.

Beasts emerged out of the jungle darkness. Monkeys were swinging from branches, birds burst from the impenetrable canopy, lizards, a black bear and even a huge gorilla appeared, its silver fur glistening under the moonlight.

Foriz backed away. 'Maybe you were right about the jungle. Maybe *I* need to take a boat home.'

'I'm assuming this is unusual?' said Livia. It was always worth confirming a hypothesis with hard evidence.

'You're an elf. Can't you just . . . sing them a song or something? Everyone knows how good you all are with animals.'

'I've a better idea,' said Livia, glancing over her shoulder. 'Run!'

CHAPTER 5
TARIQ

It was a relief to get away from everyone. And that chair! How could anyone think that was comfortable? Tariq's backside ached!

Livia and Artos were city folk. All these trees freaked them out. They wanted pavements, street lights, the hustle and bustle of carts and wagons, and the endless chatter of ten thousand voices. As he wound his way towards the shore, at long last Tariq felt he could properly relax and return to being himself as he'd been when he lived by the river.

The wind whispered. What was it trying to tell him? There was a picture, a tale, in the tree's shadow on the wall of a nearby building. The scent of the flowers triggered slumbering memories . . . Of what? Or when? There was part of him that felt he'd been here before. He was glimpsing visions of the future and also memories of a past that didn't belong to him, or at least to this life.

Tariq tried to make sense of the connections, but they flowed and ebbed through him. Using the World's Egg, he'd reached out to the vastness of the sea to control the tidal wave, but here – was the Crocodile's Tear reaching out to him? If so, he wished it would be a little clearer. All he knew and felt for sure was that it was out there in Dandaka Jungle.

They were building fast, as if in a hurry to turn a collection of shacks into a new capital. Most of the buildings were still piles of planks. Some were half erected and only a few finished, fewer of stone and brick. Marius had clearly made the building of

45

his mansion a priority, but almost everyone else lived in tents.

Or cages.

Cages were lined up along the docks, waiting to be shipped off to buyers back in Ethrial or beyond: monkeys, bears, mewling tiger cubs and plenty of vividly coloured birds. The cages were too small. The more you could pack into a ship's hull the better.

Why keep an animal like that? It didn't make any sense. You had a dog to guard the camp, or cats to keep the house mouse-free, or an eagle to hunt with. They weren't pets; they were *allies*. But the rest? Leave them alone. These wild creatures were all destined for life in cages. No life at all.

But there was worse to come.

The tiger skin was stretched across a frame. Beside it was a pile of other animal skins waiting to be cleaned, treated.

Rats nibbled at the globules of flesh that had been scraped off and tossed into the water. The mud was stained red. An old man sat on a stool, whistling as he worked the skin with a blade.

He saw Tariq and smiled. 'Beautiful, isn't it?'

'It looked better on the tiger.'

The man laughed.

Tariq put his satchel to the side and pulled off his tunic, letting it drop beside the bag. Then he kicked off his boots and buried his toes in the squelchy mud. Just like back when he was living by the river, back when life was all about fishing, swimming and feasts round the campfire with the rest of the clan.

He was a long way away from that life now. Would he ever return to it? Back in Ethrial, the other river folk were making new lives for themselves. Some were turning their talents to boat-building, others embracing brand-new opportunities within the capital. Nani was trying to settle down, having got a small cottage by one of the rivers that ran into the countless canals of Ethrial. He'd left her tending her herb garden and feeding the chickens.

Tariq missed his grandmother. If she were here, she'd know what to do. She always did.

He might be far from his old home, but at least he could have a swim. A moment later Tariq was wading in, cooling down from the steamy heat of the jungle. Under he went, pushing his way through the water and the tall seaweed.

Tariq swam past the boats with their slimy barnacle-encrusted hulls. Silver-scaled fish darted past, suddenly changing direction with a twitch of their tails. Crabs searched amongst the coral on the sea floor.

This underwater world was somewhere he could escape to. Maybe this trip wouldn't be so bad if he took a dip at the end of every day to get away from everyone just for a while. It was so peaceful down—

The water surged, buffeting him into a nearby boat. Tariq scraped his bare back against the underside of its hull, and bubbles burst from his lips as he felt the skin tear. He surfaced, gasping and circling.

There was something else in the water, something big.

Moonlight shone on rows of thick knobbly scales as they broke the surface – row on row, all along a broad back and down a thick tail. It moved with languid bestial power. It was comfortable, the way something would be that had lived here for a long, long time.

Could this be the monster crocodile? It had to be!

The beast was heading towards a small fishing boat bobbing in the sea a hundred metres from the shore. A lantern hung from the single mast, and there were nets drying from the rigging. The fisherman had decided to take advantage of the cooler sea breeze and sleep out.

A gigantic claw rose out of the water.

The hull splintered as if made of balsa wood, and the whole boat tilted to the side. The fisherman on deck didn't even have time to scream as a second claw smashed effortlessly through the wooden planks.

Even as the small boat, reduced to wreckage in a few moments, began to sink, the true danger was still to come.

The beast's jaws broke the surface of the water, hundreds of jagged white teeth glistening in the moonlight. A great red tongue, as thick as Tariq's body, unrolled, ready to take in the debris of the broken boat . . . and its crew.

The fisherman dived overboard just as the crocodile's jaws surrounded the remains of the hull and snapped shut with such power that the boat crumbled. The deck, the hull, the spars that framed it, all broke with that one irresistible snap.

From its snout to the tip of its tail it had to be over twenty metres long. It was a nightmare of a beast: huge, ancient, its scales scarred and oily black. Its tiny eyes glowed sulphurous yellow as it shook its head, working its meal of wood down its abysmal gullet.

Then Tariq saw the fisherman. He was swimming frantically towards shore, his face pale with terror.

The crocodile saw him too.

'Come on!' Tariq yelled. 'This way!'

The gigantic reptile sank under the surface, then the surface rippled as it began to swim towards its next victim, using its great tail to propel it through the water with easy, unstoppable might.

The fisherman wasn't going to make it.

Not without Tariq's help.

His spiritstone, the World's Egg, was back on land. But could he control the elements without it? Just a little? It was worth a try.

He took another deep breath and went under, sinking down till his toes touched the silt, giving him that connection. There was no way he could stop the crocodile; it was too powerful. But he could distract it . . .

The silt stirred. At first Tariq just drifted across the sea bottom, but then swirled, rising higher, creating a dense cloud within the water, enough to hide the fisherman from the monster chasing him below.

Tariq forced more silt to mix with the sea until he couldn't see anything. If he was blind, then so was the crocodile.

Would it be enough?

Tariq broke the surface – the fisherman an arm's length from him. Both turned for land and swam desperately. Soon Tariq's toes touched the bottom, and then he and the fisherman were scrabbling on to the land.

He looked over his shoulder.

Blinded by the silt, the crocodile slammed into another boat anchored near the shore. Its instinct was to destroy everything in its path, so in its fury it slammed both claws into the hull, shattering the thick wood and dragging the entire vessel down into the water, where it tore it into slivers and smashed it apart with its tail.

But crocodiles weren't confined to water.

Tariq stumbled to his feet even as the crocodile twisted its immense head and their eyes met. That look was . . . knowing.

Panting, Tariq grabbed hold of the fisherman and pushed him up the slope. 'We need to run.' Then, a moment before he raced after him, Tariq grabbed his satchel and looped it over his arm. Even with the monster snapping at his heels, there was no way he was forgetting the World's Egg.

The demon crocodile hissed through its teeth, pausing in its destruction. It gave the boat one last blow with a contemptuous flick of its tail.

Then it started towards the shore.

CHAPTER 6
ARTOS

Artos's room had a balcony facing the town. Marius had clearly wanted to make a good impression. Not that he cared for Artos, but he cared for his father, Councillor Lugus, the head of the Ethrial Council.

My first command, thought Artos as he stood on the balcony, gazing out at the town and all that needed to be done.

The pier needed extending. Artos would build a

lighthouse up on the hill to the west. Lord Marius would see the sense in that. More ships meant more profits.

He slapped the mosquito at his neck. Why did they find him so tasty?

Artos had never understood why his father had been so keen on building, on expanding. Ethrial was too crowded. But here there were no limits.

Maybe he was more like his father than he liked to admit.

They'd start on the wall tomorrow. He'd mark out the line, pick the best place for the main gate, with a watch tower either side and taller towers at the ends. They'd need to clear the jungle back from the wall . . . a hundred metres? That would give the guards plenty of warning if anyone, or anything, approached.

And what about the guards? The thugs Marius used had to be replaced. New Ethrial needed the Silver Guard.

Other than Febian, that is. He wasn't happy about Artos being here, but their goal was the same: to develop and protect the new colony. They would work together because they had to. The Silver Guard kept any rivalry out of sight. Against the outside world they were always united, shields locked together against all dangers. He hated to admit it, but Febian was a good warrior. Great even. The two of them were rising stars within the Silver Guard; there was no way they'd be able to avoid each other. Their careers would be bound together for a long, long time.

Artos sat down heavily on his bed and pulled off his boots, then reached for his sword resting against the bedpost. You were expected to always have it within reach, no matter what. He shook it out of its scabbard.

The small lantern hanging from the ceiling shone on the silvery surface of Cleaver. When Artos tilted it into the light just a little – like this – he could see the ripple pattern on the steel. Now that was proper korrish craftsmanship, designed for korrish hands. It was chunky and heavy, the sort of weapon you could hack with, not like the delicate needles the elves fought with.

He fished out the whetstone and settled down to sharpening the blade. It helped him find some calm.

A chattering noise made him look towards the open window and the balcony. A monkey sat on the railings, its tail curved round the wrought iron, its long fingers picking at a nut shell. It wedged it between its teeth and the shell cracked, but its shiny black eyes were focused on Artos.

Artos rested the sword on the bed. 'If you want anything to eat, you'd better go downstairs.'

The monkey peered in, then hopped on to the floor and entered the room. It searched around, poking into Artos's open chest, tugging at the neatly folded pile of clothes.

'Hey! Be careful with those! I don't have any nuts in there!'

Its search completed, the monkey crossed the room, acting as if it owned the place, and jumped up on to the bedpost opposite Artos, hands resting on its knees.

'What are you doing? You can't stay in here.'

But the monkey just turned its attention to the open window.

'What are you waiting for?' asked Artos, following its gaze. The moon was high, casting its pale light on the few tiled rooftops of New Ethrial.

And on one roof across the street the darkness was alive. It broke free of the shadows and prowled across the tiles, utterly silent, its amber eyes simmering like furnace flames.

A panther.

The size of it! How could it move so silently? Not a single tile shifted under its pads and its long black tail swished from side to side as it searched.

For what?

Artos's bed creaked as the monkey tossed one of his pillows off the bed. It wriggled under the blanket, its own tail vanishing beneath the embroidered wool.

Wings flapped overhead and a dozen birds swooped across the star-sprinkled sky. Vultures, eagles, even a few kingfishers with their dazzling feathers, glided past on the night wind. They spread out over the cluster of buildings, settling on roofs, branches and even the spars of the sailing ships anchored out in the bay.

As Artos watched from his balcony, more animals crept through the empty streets and dark alleys between the warehouses and huts, predator and prey side by side. A deer sniffed at a doorway while a leopard padded across the rooftop of the building opposite the mansion.

It didn't make any sense. Leopards hunted deer. Why was it ignoring its natural prey?

There was activity in the bay. Someone was shouting. One of the boats anchored on the docks was now a floating wreck and something big and scaly was moving in the black water, heading towards the shore.

Artos grabbed his sword. The monkey hissed at him, then sprang over his head and scarpered out of the window, leaping from the railings into a tree just beyond. The leaves rustled as it disappeared deep within.

A roar swept across the night. It echoed off the roofs and the alleyway walls. The great panther raised its head to the moon and roared again, a deep chest-powered summoning of the wild things of Dandaka.

The birds suddenly took flight. They swooped low over the town while monkeys scurried over the moonlit roofs and into open windows. Screams and cries rose, one after the other, from the invaded buildings.

The leopard leapt across the width of the street and through the window of the room beside his.

Artos ran to his bedroom door and swung it open. 'We're under attack!'

They were in the courtyard. A dozen monkeys and a massive silver-haired gorilla. It had been squatting on the dining table, picking at the leftovers, but now turned its huge head towards Artos. The giant ape bared its teeth as it leapt across the courtyard and pounded its way up the stairs, bellowing its challenge.

Artos tightened both hands on his sword hilt. 'Come on, then . . .'

CHAPTER 7
TARIQ

'We're being attacked! Everyone lock your doors!' yelled Tariq as he ran up the Grand Avenue.

It was chaos. While the crocodile was demolishing the docks, there were monkeys tearing at the thatched roofs, screaming in a frenzy, as two bears roared at a squad of trembling guards, beating away their flimsy spears with huge forepaws. Birds swooped out of the trees, shrieking and slashing with their talons. Tariq jumped over an enormous boa constrictor as it wound its way out of an alleyway. Farm animals – goats and sheep and chickens – ran around, getting underfoot, in a total panic. Locals waved torches or shook their brooms, trying to frighten off the rampaging beasts. But to no avail. The jungle animals were being driven by some strange, furious purpose.

'Tariq! Tariq!'

Livia – with Foriz – stumbled towards him. Livia was reloading a fire-spitter while Foriz had her chain wrapped round her fist as a weapon.

They turned at the sound of a thunderous crunch. The colossal crocodile was demolishing one of the warehouses with lashes of its trunk-like tail.

'We've got to get out of here,' said Foriz, panting heavily.

Livia shook her head. 'And go where? The jungle? Be my guest.'

Tariq looked around at the riot. Someone had thrown their torch at a pack of jackals, missed, and now one of the houses was alight – the thatch burning hungrily.

'The whole town's going to burn down unless we do something,' he said.

Foriz waved at the sky. 'Can't you magic up a rainstorm?'

'In theory . . .' He'd commanded a tidal wave, so knew the World's Egg gave him control over the elements, but there wasn't a cloud in the sky. He wouldn't know where to start.

Foriz huffed. 'Some seer you are.'

'We need a more practical answer,' said Tariq. 'Where's Artos?'

'Back in the mansion,' replied Livia.

'We need him out here,' said Tariq. 'Someone needs to take command of the fighting and I don't see Febian anywhere.'

Livia nodded and sprinted off towards Marius's mansion.

Tariq turned to face Foriz. 'Looks like it's just you and me.'

'No, it's just you.' Then she blew him a kiss and ran off.

'Oh, bye then. I'll just do this by . . . FORIZ!'

A huge panther had spotted her and was leaping from rooftop to rooftop, chasing her.

'Foriz, watch out!' he yelled.

But she couldn't hear him over the bedlam or else was ignoring him.

Tariq tightened his satchel across his shoulder and ran after her.

The panther moved with supernatural grace, slipping in and out of the ever-changing shadows from the spreading fires, the flames reflecting in its golden gaze. It was almost on her.

Tariq gritted his teeth as he pushed his legs harder, splashing through the slippery mud and closing in on the fleeing young woman until he was right at her back. 'Foriz!'

Tariq leapt. So did the panther.

Its claws scraped across his back just as he knocked Foriz down. They landed with a bone-jarring huff while the panther twisted in mid-air to land with barely a sound, facing them. It bared its teeth and growled softly.

Tariq rolled to his feet and Foriz scrambled up, loosening her chain.

'You go left, I'll go right,' she whispered. 'When it attacks one, the other goes in.'

'Who will it attack?' Tariq asked.

'The weakest.' Foriz glanced at him. 'That'll be you.'

'Oh.' Those teeth would finish him off with a single bite.

An eagle swooped over them to land on a rooftop. It spread out its dark brown wings, ruffling its feathers as it settled to watch. Its golden eyes peered at him curiously.

The panther's muscles quivered as it prepared to pounce.

Where was Artos? Now would be the perfect moment for him to come charging in, sword aloft.

But there was no Artos. It was just down to them. Tariq half expected Foriz to run off while the panther tore him to pieces. She didn't owe him anything; in fact, he'd ruined her life back in Ethrial. She probably blamed him for being shipped and, truth be told, she might even be right to.

What should he do? Roll to the side when the panther—

As it leapt at him, its roar froze Tariq to the spot. Foriz screamed as she swung her chain, catching the beast along the ribs, enough to knock it off target so it slammed into Tariq with its shoulder, sending him tumbling.

The eagle swooped off its perch, talons extended.

The animals were fighting together! How was that even possible?

The eagle struck Foriz, clawing at her, trying to get to her face, while the panther sprang to its feet and spun to face him. Tariq backed away and grabbed a weapon, a burning piece of wood that had fallen from a nearby building.

The panther edged closer while Foriz and the eagle fought.

'Come on, then,' Tariq snarled, trying his best to mimic Artos's ferociousness.

The panther paused. Maybe it was scared of the fire?

'Tarrrriq?' it growled.

Tariq shook his head. 'Say . . . say that again.'

'Tarrrriq.' The jaguar stared at him, eyes widening. 'Tarrrriq!'

The eagle broke away and circled over them. It shrieked once more and landed on the ground, covering itself with its wings. The bird shook and . . . began changing. The feathers sank into its body as it began to grow bigger, while its wings altered shape into something more like . . . arms?

The panther stepped closer. 'Tariq.' It hunched over and shivered.

Foriz stared. 'I don't believe it.'

The black fur faded into its skin. The limbs resculpted themselves into arms and legs. The fierce muzzle retreated into the skull as it transformed into something altogether more human.

'Tariq. It's you.'

The panther was gone. In its place was a woman crouching on all fours, staring at him in wonder. She touched a long fang dangling from her necklace. 'It's really you.'

'You've grown, boy.'

Out of the shadows, where the eagle had been, stood a man: bearded, muscular, with eagle feathers tied to his long black hair. 'What do you think, Miriam?'

The woman stood up and laughed. 'I'm as shocked as you are, Nazir. Come here, Tariq!' She held out her arms. 'Give your mother a hug.'

CHAPTER 8
LIVIA

Livia barged back into the mansion. Monkeys swung from the railings and servants battled them with brooms and frying pans. A leopard was on the dining table, a roast chicken in its jaws, and a four-metre-long boa constrictor slinked across the floor as Febian fended it off with a chair in one hand, his silver sword in the other.

'Where's Artos?' Livia yelled at Febian.

'Can't you see I'm busy?' he snapped back.

Then she heard a thunderous bellow from the courtyard. There was no mistaking that voice.

Artos was on the steps leading up to the bedrooms, swinging his broadsword, while a great silver-furred gorilla towered over him, its fists the size of boulders.

'Duck!' Livia shouted. She pointed the fire-spitter at the gorilla and pulled the trigger.

She juddered from head to toe as a jet of blue flame erupted from the barrel mouth, washing the darkness with brilliant light and hurling half a dozen fiery pellets across the courtyard.

The pellets burst as they struck the gorilla's massive torso, scattering flaming ash over its thick silver fur. It roared as the hair caught fire, and instead of crashing on top of Artos the ape tumbled over the banister on to the floor below, landing with a heavy thud. It rolled to its feet, beating at the flames even as it fled.

Artos grinned and saluted the elf with a flourish of his sword.

Others were spilling out of their bedrooms. Lord Marius yelled for his guards while brandishing a copper-plated bedpan. Febian drove off the giant snake, then turned his attention to the leopard.

'Where's Tariq?' asked Artos as he joined her.

Livia reloaded the fire-spitter. 'Back out there.'

'We need to find him before he gets himself in trouble.' Artos flipped his sword from one hand to the other.

Livia arched an eyebrow. 'You practise that a lot?'

He flipped the sword back. 'Quite a bit actually.'

She bowed. 'After you, *Sir* Artos.'

They ran outside to find beasts rampaging through New Ethrial. Vultures tore the thatch off roofs, there was a bear ripping down the door to one of the warehouses and a pack of jackals prowled the shadows. There were more animals gathered round the cages at the seafront. Birds, a grey wolf and monkeys were clambering over them. The wolf locked its jaws round the wooden bars of one and a second later they shattered. The tiger cubs within scampered free, racing inland towards the edge of the jungle before vanishing into the dense foliage.

'They're freeing them,' said Artos, awestruck. 'I know I'm city born, but that's not normal, is it?'

The monkeys were now picking at the knots holding the cages closed. The bigger beasts, including a giant crocodile, merely tore the wooden bars apart. Wolf cubs yapped as they were freed, parrots flapped their bright green wings as they fled back into the jungle, and cage after cage was methodically destroyed. Livia gazed into the sky as birds of paradise fluttered away into the darkness. The night was filled with the wild roars, howls and cries of the living, raging jungle.

'What's happening?'

Lord Marius had run into the street in silk pyjamas and his feathered hat, waving his bedpan. He gazed at the rows of broken cages. 'My beautiful animals! I had buyers for each of them! Those tiger cubs were worth a fortune. Now they're all gone!'

Livia watched the cubs race off into the darkness. 'So it's not all bad news, eh?'

Lord Marius glared at her. 'How do you think your precious guild gets financed? Who paid for your precious Harvester?'

Let him rant. Livia turned her attention towards the dark wall of green on the outskirts of the town, the barrier between this new civilisation and the ancient wild.

The ground began to shake. The trees swayed violently. Bats burst from the jungle, flapping erratically and shrieking in big black-winged clouds.

'Uh-oh,' said Artos, grabbing her hand.

One moment the trees were swaying, the next they were trampled underfoot as elephants stampeded into New Ethrial.

They smashed down a row of hovels without effort. One ploughed into the corner of a new brick building, demolishing the scaffolding and bringing the wall down. It trumpeted with joy as it emerged from the cloud of dust. People fled their homes in panic, running in all directions.

'Where is Tariq?' yelled Artos. But no one was listening.

A huge vulture swooped down and ripped Marius's hat from his head. It cawed mockingly as, with a great beat of its wings, it rose back into the night with the hat clutched between its talons.

'First rank, shoot!' shouted Febian to a line of guards. Crossbows twanged as steel-tipped quarrels flashed through the air. An elephant roared as several arrows buried themselves into its flank.

Torches flared. People rushed in, spears and nets at the ready.

A roar shook the night sky, louder and more powerful than the sounds of battle. The trees themselves rustled, as if they were under its command. The roar rose again, so full of power and pride that it raised the hairs along Livia's nape.

The beasts responded with their own cries, the elephants lifting their trunks to trumpet their response. The giant crocodile smashed down a row of huts before slipping back into the water and disappearing with barely a ripple.

Livia watched, mouth open, as the animals retreated. Artos pulled her into a doorway as a pack of wolves charged past.

The Battle of New Ethrial was over. And as Livia gazed, stunned, at the wreckage, people wandered around the remains of their homes, of their livelihoods. Some were injured; they'd need taking care of.

But where was Tariq?

CHAPTER 9
TARIQ

Tariq stumbled through the humid darkness, tripping over roots and being slapped by hanging vines over and over until he was dripping with mud and covered in scratches. The panther led the way, pausing regularly to make sure Tariq and Foriz weren't falling too far behind. It growled impatiently while the eagle flew overhead, hidden beyond the dense canopy, piercing the ominous jungle with its high-pitched shrieks.

He shouldn't think of the panther as 'it', but 'she'.
Mum.

Both his parents were seers, gifted with a deep supernatural understanding of nature, of the wild. But beast forms? That was straight out of the oldest legends.

The panther – Mum – stopped on top of a mossy tree trunk that lay across their path. She swished her tail back and forth, waiting for the pair to catch up. Leaves rustled above and the eagle, Dad, swooped down through the canopy to settle on a bough, sending a family of bats fleeing.

Tariq turned round as he heard a sudden cry and splash.

Foriz lay coughing and spluttering in a greenish puddle.

Tariq held out his hand. 'Here.'

'I can manage,' snapped Foriz, crawling out of the mud on her hands and knees before slowly getting to her feet and spitting out more stagnant water. 'Where are they taking us?'

There hadn't been time to find out, not amidst the chaos of the attack. No time for Tariq to think, just do as Mum had told him. He looked back the way they'd come, trying to discern the route they'd taken. Impossible. The foliage seemed to have closed behind them. The jungle kept its secrets. There was no way he'd find his way back to the others.

'Where are we going?' Tariq asked.

'Somewhere safe,' said Dad. Eagle no more, he swung down off the bough and embraced Tariq.

It had been so long. So long he'd almost forgotten what it was like hugging his dad.

He'd only come up to his waist the night his parents had been banished from the clan. Now Tariq was at his shoulder, but his dad's big arms and big chest with its mighty heart were just the same. And Dad's smell. That was the same too . . . but richer, more alive somehow.

Mum joined them, and Tariq, for the first time in years, felt . . . *safe*. Taken care of. His parents were here. He shook, letting go of everything he'd been holding on to – all the worries, all the fears, all the hopes he'd been bearing without even realising. He could stop being the answer to everyone's problems now. He was Tariq again. Just Tariq.

Dad's beard was rough against his forehead as he pulled Tariq back. His deep brown eyes gleamed. 'Let me have a proper look at you, son. You're no longer a boy now but a grown—'

Foriz spat loudly. 'That's all very moving, but I need to know where we're going and what your plans are. Or is this just about the hugs? In which case point me to the sea and I'll make my way from there.'

Mum wiped a tear away, and was still grinning as she smiled at Tariq, her fangs not yet changed back. 'The jungle's too dangerous, young lady. You'll stay with us.'

'For how long?'

'As long as necessary,' Mum growled.

Foriz turned pale. She was scared. Tariq hadn't thought it possible.

He had so many questions, like how had his parents learnt to shape-change? What had happened to them after they'd been exiled? But there was one question more than any other that ached inside his heart.

'I've been waiting so long. Why didn't you come and get me?' asked Tariq. 'I thought you'd forgotten all about me.'

All those nights he'd cried, missing them. Nani had done her best to comfort him, but a grandmother couldn't replace your parents, no matter how much you loved her and she loved you.

Dad sighed and gave Tariq an extra squeeze. 'The first few years were hard, hard and dangerous. We were vagabonds, son, barely making it from one month to the next. No life for you. Once we settled here we sent word, hoping someone would tell you where we were, but the river clan had moved on. The people we reached couldn't find you. All the places we once knew had been drowned by dams, the old rivers rerouted. What happened?'

'A lot of things,' said Tariq. The clan leaving for the city of Ethrial. The river clan being accused of bringing disease into the city. His visions of destruction. Using the World's Egg to stop the tidal wave . . . He patted the satchel, checking the Egg was still there.

'It's a long tale, Dad.'

'I want you to tell us *everything*,' said Dad, smiling. 'We've all the time in the world.'

He'd missed sharing tales by the fireside. There was no better way to spend the evenings. 'Where are we headed?'

'Xibalba,' said Dad.

Tariq stared at him. 'Xibalba? I thought it was a legend.'

Mum winked. 'You'll love it.'

Xibalba. The great temple of the seers, where they would study and learn to use their gifts. Seers had been far more powerful in the distant past, back when the spiritstones had been kept together. Tariq knew that each stone amplified the power of the others, their energies radiating across the world so any seer, no matter how far away, could tap into that power. He'd sat round the campfire listening to tales of the ancient seers who could rearrange mountain peaks, raise forests overnight and bring peace with merely a word and smile. All these abilities were learnt at Xibalba.

He took a fruit off the tree next to them and handed it to Foriz.

She frowned. 'What is it?'

'A mango. It's sweet.'

Foriz bit into it, skin and all. She ate it with urgency, as if she'd not tasted anything sweet in months. The juice ran down her fingers, along her arms and she licked the sticky syrup off her bare skin, then set to nibbling every piece of flesh off the stone, sucking it clean. At last she wiped her face with the back of her hand. 'Not bad.'

'I didn't know you'd been shipped. I'm sorry I didn't help you when I could have.'

Foriz tossed the stone away. 'Sorry? You looked after yourself. I'd have done the same if our positions had been swapped.'

Mum came alongside, chewing on her own mango. 'Being a panther's all well and good, but they can't enjoy mangoes. Tongues like sandpaper!'

He still couldn't believe it. 'How did you learn to shape-change?'

Mum paused and glanced back at Dad, who shrugged. 'You might as well tell him, Miriam.'

Mum wiped her mouth. 'We were taught alongside the others.'

'Others?' Tariq looked back. 'Were all the animals that attacked the town seers like you?'

Mum shook her head. 'No, only a handful. Most are just beasts of the jungle. They're our friends, all willing to help when the need's great. The world's a different place once you speak the Wild Tongue. Every animal becomes your kin.'

'Wild Tongue?!' Tariq exclaimed. 'I thought that was just a myth. But then there's a lot that I thought was just myth until tonight. So you can speak with animals too? That's amazing! Could you teach me?'

She grinned at him. 'All in good time, Tariq. There are plenty of other seers gathered here in Dandaka. That's where she made her home.'

'She?' asked Tariq. 'Who?'

Mum laughed. 'Imix, of course.'

'*The* Imix?' It wasn't possible. 'But . . . she lived a thousand years ago. She must be long dead by now.'

Dad grinned at him. 'Oh, she's alive. And she's *very* keen to meet you.'

*

The jungle was never silent. But there was a difference between the quiet murmurs of the night and the rising orchestra of the day. They'd walked through the night; Tariq had been too excited to rest and Foriz too keen to get as far from New Ethrial as possible. As the morning mists evaporated, so the music of the jungle rose out of the treetops, from the caves and pools and impenetrable foliage. Tariq had been born in the forest, but the jungle was the grandparent of the woodlands that had been his home, and the life here was richer, denser, ancient with deeper roots.

This is where it all began. He could feel it.

After the birds sang in the morning, Tariq heard the distant roars of big cats. They were proclaiming their territories, warning interlopers away from their kingdoms. Monkeys chattered overhead as they swung from branch to branch, nibbling at fruit and gathering in family groups to feast, gossip and preen. A red and yellow macaw glided through the emerald canopy.

Yet behind the activity he detected a presence, half hidden but quietly calling him. It made the hairs on the back of his neck stand up and raised goosebumps along his bare arms. It was like a low growl, too deep to be heard, but it could be felt right in the bones.

The Crocodile's Tear was close, he was sure of it.

Hidden amongst the wilderness was the work of mortals. First were signs of an ancient road. Weeds, flowers and trees had sprouted between pitted, weathered flagstones, yet the path was there. It was marked by tall stone slabs. These towering obsidian blocks were carved with legends of when the elemental lords, mortals and beasts had lived side by side in peace – the days when the spiritstones had blessed the world with harmony. They depicted creatures from myths. Winged horses. Birds that could carry elephants in their claws. Serpents who encircled the seas.

Foriz stood beside him. 'An age of monsters.'

Why did she always have to spoil everything? Tariq found the tales wonderful.

'You believe your parents?' she asked. 'About Imix and Xibalba?'

Of course – Foriz had been raised on the same tales. Her parents had been folk of the mountain clans, even though she'd spent most of her life in the city of Ethrial amongst smugglers and thieves.

'Why shouldn't I?' Tariq asked, a little angry that she thought his parents would lie to him. 'You saw them shape-change. Someone taught them to do that, someone very powerful and wise. Who else but Imix, the greatest seer of all time?'

Foriz smirked. 'Imix was the greatest thief of all time.'

'Then you and her have plenty in common.'

And if anyone knew about the second spiritstone, the Crocodile's Tear, it would be Imix. Could his quest already be over? Tariq tried to control his excitement. He'd found his parents! They could shape-change! It was all too good to be true.

Mum waved at him from up ahead. 'Come and see, Tariq.'

Water sparkled through the trees; there was a lake ahead of them. A lake . . . and people. Smoke scented the air along with the smell of damp soil and the perfume of flowers. A faint sound of activity, of sawing, hammering and laughter, drifted across the water.

Tariq emerged from the trees and joined his parents at the edge of the lake.

Canoes floated on a vast expanse of water. People swam and fished. On the opposite shore stood a city. Towering statues of beastfolk lined the streets, and there was a central stepped pyramid with the rising sun crowning its summit. People were dressed in animal skins, in feathers, in dyed cloth made from hemp and other plants. Wildly colourful birds swooped over the towering monolithic houses that were carved with extraordinary care and detail.

Dad put his arm round Tariq's shoulders and squeezed. 'Welcome to Xibalba.'

CHAPTER 10
LIVIA

'We need to find Tariq!' Livia declared. 'The longer we delay, the less chance we have of finding him!'

By dawn they'd realised the extent of the damage. Many of the houses were wrecked, all but one of the warehouses a smouldering ruin, the captured beasts gone and half the boats in the docks now just so much flotsam.

It would take weeks to repair, but the town of New Ethrial had to wait its turn. All efforts were focused on reinstating Lord Marius's mansion to its former glory first.

While half the townsfolk were making do in tents and shacks made of driftwood and palm-frond roofs, Lord Marius already had the walls being repainted with fresh murals.

'And I want those windows replaced by tonight,' he said. A dozen servants scurried back and forth while he sat at a table in the courtyard like some petty king. He straightened his lace cuffs. 'What were you saying, m'dear?'

Artos leaned over the table, his big knuckles resting on the polished Dandaka wood. 'She was saying we need to rescue our friend right now. I need ten of your soldiers and a scout, a poacher or a hunter. Anyone who knows the jungle.'

Lord Marius scowled. 'No one knows the jungle. You venture too deep in there and you're not coming back. If last night's disaster demonstrated anything, it's that Dandaka isn't for civilised folk like us.'

'What about Tariq?' Livia asked.

Lord Marius shrugged. 'I can't spare anyone.'

Livia looked round and caught sight of Febian as he stepped through the front door. 'Febian! Get some warriors together. We need to save Tariq.'

Febian sat down at the table and helped himself to a bunch of grapes. 'I'm not losing the men on a fool's errand. Tariq's on his own.'

Livia glared at him. 'Tariq is one of us. You're duty-bound to help him. It's the law of Ethrial!'

'In case you didn't realise, we're not in Ethrial. Here I am under the command of the governor.' Febian bowed towards the pompous elf. 'And he quite sensibly will not waste his resources on a rescue mission doomed to fail.'

'Quite right,' said Lord Marius. 'And your job is to get the Harvester working. We've set it up at the edge of the jungle. The sooner we get those trees chopped down, the sooner we can start rebuilding. That's what's important. Your mentor, Lady Fausta, surely would agree.'

'No one touches my machine except me,' Livia replied. 'It's dangerous.'

Febian chuckled. 'That's exactly what I was

thinking. All those spinning blades. It's a shame we didn't have it last night. Chop, chop, chop . . .'

Livia glared at him. 'It's not a weapon.'

Febian just smirked.

Artos looked at Febian across the table, and it was good there was two metres between them otherwise Livia had a feeling Artos would have done something unpleasant to the arrogant guard. Artos stuck out his jaw and his blue eyes seemed to glow beneath his heavy brow. 'Tariq is my friend. I'm not leaving him to the beasts, or whatever it was that attacked us last night.'

Livia grinned. 'I'll start packing.'

*

The Harvester. It was a beautiful piece of engineering.

It was parked at the edge of town, all gleaming and brand new, and every blade as bright as silver. Livia pressed her hand against the engine. Warm. She checked the dial. The pressure was midway, exactly right. Too low and it wouldn't have enough chopping power, too high and it would break

90

apart. A few of the townsfolk had gathered round to admire it and she'd loved explaining how it worked. If this trial went well, the Guild would ship a second over next season.

A village today. Then a town. One day a city. Now that was progress.

And it all started with this machine.

She settled into the driving seat and pulled the lever up.

The engine took a moment to come to life. There was a gentle shake – it was good that she'd installed springs under the seat – and then a tremble as the six blades began turning, sunlight catching their edges. The triple pair of claws clanged open and shut, eager to grab a tree or three.

They'd thought about calling it the Crab. That's what had inspired her. She'd been down at the docks helping Lady Fausta with a new prototype of the Seahorse and they'd been discussing farming, how inefficient it all was. Lumberjacks to chop the trees down, horses to pull up the stumps. Chop and pull. Chop and pull. Livia's attention had been caught by a crab, using its claws to pull seaweed out of the sand. She'd started sketching right there and then.

If you squinted, you could see it was a crab, sort of. Biggest claws at the front, then the medium-sized ones, then the smallest behind. Each claw had two spinning blades so it could chop and pull at the same time. Now that was efficiency!

The blades started whirring. She released the handbrake and pressed down on the pedal.

They'd decided against wheels. Instead the machine had six legs, just like a crab, with huge pads for feet, perfect for mud and uneven ground. The Harvester took a few steps forward. The crowd oohed and aahed. Someone cheered.

It was working!

'Most impressive,' said Febian. He cast an admiring gaze over the six blades. 'Tempered steel? Must be as sharp as any sword.'

'They're rust-resistant and don't need sharpening,' said Livia.

Febian's cold grey eyes glistened. 'You really have thought of everything.'

Livia pulled the brake back on and turned the engine off. 'Do not touch anything, Febian. I mean it.'

'Or what?' he asked, a hand lightly resting on his sword hilt. 'You'll poke me with your quill?'

'What's going on?' asked Artos, looking from one to the other. He huffed loudly as he gazed at the Harvester. 'That's a lot of blades, Livia.'

Not him too. Didn't they understand that it wasn't a weapon? But to a warrior everything was a weapon.

Artos gestured towards the river. 'The boat's waiting. Come on.'

Livia dismounted and watched as the rumbling machine gently settled. The smell of vulcanite smoke reminded her of home. She put her palm against the engine, feeling its warmth, as if it was a living beast.

It had all started with a few sketches and calculations, then crafting a few small working prototypes, toys really, first powered by clockwork, then with a tiny vulcanite engine, little more than candle. Now here it stood, the brass and steel bright in the sunlight of a new day.

Febian drummed his fingers on one of the big blades. 'Don't worry, Livia. I'll look after it.'

*

'Is all this necessary?!' exclaimed Artos as they reached the riverbank.

Livia frowned as she looked at the neat pile of equipment waiting to be lifted on to the boat. 'It's the bare essentials.'

Artos sighed loudly, his fists resting on his hips, which Livia was learning was a bad sign. 'So what's this?'

Livia put her hand protectively over the old wooden crate criss-crossed with reinforcing bands of metal. 'My toolbox. There is no way I'm going anywhere without it.'

He pointed to the big leather satchel. 'I thought that was your toolbox.'

'That's my tool *bag*. Completely different.'

He held up a smaller canvas satchel. 'And this?'

'My pocket tool kit. Also essential. In case I lose the other two.'

Artos bit his lip. 'And who did you expect to carry all this?'

'We could share it between us,' said Livia.

'Meaning I'd carry all the heavy stuff?'

'That's very kind of you,' said Livia. 'Honestly, with this new strap arrangement you'll hardly feel the weight at all.'

'I have my own stuff, Livia!' He slapped his hand on his sword. 'This. Then there's the tent. Then there's the food. Then there's the water. Also essential.'

'We're following a river. I think there'll be plenty of water.' Livia smiled broadly. 'See? Cut your baggage by half already!'

Artos looked at the river suspiciously. 'Have you seen what's in the water?'

'But we might need to . . . build something? At short notice?'

Artos slapped at a mosquito nibbling his neck. 'We don't know what we're doing, do we? I'm used to cobblestones under my feet, not finding snakes in my boots.'

'There's nothing to worry about.' Livia gazed out at the vast jungle upriver. 'I've got a book by Johannus the famous explorer. He gives plenty of tips for surviving in the wilderness. I've highlighted a few important sections . . .'

'You think you'll have all you need from a book?'

Livia frowned at him. 'Of course. I've learnt everything from books.'

Artos drew his sword and marked a neat circle in the mud. 'Books don't teach you how to use this. Or survive out there.'

'So what's your plan, then?' Livia asked. The truth was, she was starting to agree with Artos. She'd packed all this stuff because she didn't know what she was up against. She dipped her hand in Left-Hand-Side Pocket Four and took out a small device. 'I've a compass.'

'That's more like it. What's in that other pocket?'

She pulled out her torch.

Artos nodded. 'Good. We travel light, Livia. As light and as fast as we can. I spoke to one of the hunters and he found Tariq's tracks, along with another's, probably Foriz. It looked like they were following the river. There's a big lake upriver, so that's where we'll head. We follow it, find Tariq and come straight back. No stopping to draw flowers or catch strange insects. So that box over there . . .' he pointed to her air-tight sample box, '. . . that stays here.'

'What about your armour? You're going dressed like that?'

Artos plucked his tunic. 'I'm sweating enough just in this. Another tip the hunter gave me: tuck your trousers into your boots. Don't want anything that bites or stings crawling up your leg.'

'Maybe we should take this hunter friend of yours with us.'

Artos laughed. 'I offered him a hundred gold, but he just shook his head and said all the gold in Ethrial wouldn't be enough for him to go into the deep jungle. "That's the kingdom of beasts," he said, "and it's ruled by the giant crocodile".'

The beast that had almost flattened the town. Livia remembered the gleam of its teeth and the size of it as it had stomped its way along the docks, swishing its tail.

Upriver. It was a sensible plan. All creatures needed water, so it made sense they'd be based near water. But that lake sounded exactly like the sort of place a crocodile would make its home.

Artos looked at his pocket watch. 'Ten minutes and we're off. A boat will take us to the lake.'

She nodded. 'Poor Tariq. We need to find him as soon as possible. He must be having the worst time ever.'

CHAPTER 11
TARIQ

'This is amazing!' yelled Tariq across the table. He was having the best time ever!

His parents raised their jugs and he did the same, then gulped down the thick mix of banana and papaya juice. Delicious. He smacked his lips, then grabbed another grilled fish off the platter. It was his . . . fifth? Maybe he should leave room for the chicken? The smells coming from the spit turning over the fire pit were making his head spin. Everything was covered in strange spices, unlike anything he'd ever tasted before, even in Ethrial, which was meant to have food from everywhere. How could he go back to porridge after this?

The feast filled the entire square in the centre of the settlement. As evening fell, the inhabitants of Xibalba had gathered, every household bringing a plate of delicious fruit, meat or vegetables. The fires glowed and sent scented smoke into the star-scattered night, and musicians set to work with pipes, drums and songs in a language that he didn't understand but felt deep inside him. People danced, their shadows alive with joy.

Seers from all across the world had found their home here, far away from civilisation. Seers from the desert clans, from the mountains, seafarers and others from the different river clans – even a seer from the ice clans, the ones who hunted whales in the icy north. There were some as young as him, girls and boys who'd somehow followed the stories to this fabled kingdom of the seers.

Tariq had come searching for the second spiritstone, the Crocodile's Tear, but found something so much better.

These were his people. Tariq knew this feast wasn't for him, it was to celebrate the attack on New Ethrial, but once his parents had told the others who he was, the feast had turned into a celebration of another seer coming 'home' as well.

Tariq burped. Five fish was enough. He dug his fingers into the stack of grapes. 'They're huge! Does everything grow like this here?'

Mum plucked a grape off the stalk and turned it in the firelight as if it were a purple gemstone. 'What would you expect? We're seers. It's not hard to make everything . . . richer.'

Tariq thought of the World's Egg in his satchel. 'Mum, I need to show you something.'

'Hmm?'

Tariq looked around the crowd. 'Is Imix here yet? I really want to meet her.'

Mum shook her head. 'On patrol. She'll be back soon enough. Always home by dawn.'

Dad had joined them, waving a skewer with a chunk of sizzling meat. 'Try the goat. It's delicious.'

'Can we go somewhere a bit quieter?' He really didn't want to get the Egg out here, not until his parents knew what he had.

They looked at each other, their expressions suddenly serious. That was different too. They looked at him as if he was . . . an equal now.

The three of them wandered away from the feast to a quiet spot on the lakeside, beside the boats and drying nets.

'You know that our rivers flooded when they built the dam to serve Ethrial?'

Mum looked grim. 'It made me angry to think those arrogant city folk would destroy our homes. But they are greedy and care nothing for the earth.'

'The clan rowed down to the city, to try and find new lives. I met some people, good people. Artos is in the Silver Guard, Livia is an apprentice at the Guild of Artificers. We found something . . . important.'

Dad arched his eyebrow. 'What?'

Tariq flipped the satchel open and pulled out the Egg. 'This.'

Lights swirled gently within the heart of the semi-transparent stone. Blues, reds, soft yellows and greens. It was as if the elements themselves had been bound into it. Tariq could see fire flickering deep inside and hear the roar of the sea. There was the smell of fresh pine, the perfume of blossom and moist earth. Once he'd have had to concentrate to make these connections, but they became easier and easier each time he tried.

Mum's eyes widened with awe. 'The World's Egg. But . . . but how?'

'It was in Ethrial. The Artificers had used it to power their pumping station but it had been polluted, creating disease. It was trying to cleanse Ethrial in its own way.'

'And what way was that?' asked Mum.

'Er, by destroying it with a tidal wave.'

His parents looked at each other. Then Dad shrugged. 'That'll do it.'

Tariq watched the colours shift within the spiritstone. 'Things are out of balance. Ethrial was polluted by the smoke rising from its thousands of chimneys and all the factories. The air was thick with ash sometimes, and it was only getting worse. The spiritstone was trying to fix things.'

Dad nodded thoughtfully. 'That was their original purpose. The spiritstones were created by the gods, or so they say, to maintain the balance between all aspects of nature. The World's Egg could alter the elements, whether fire, earth, air or water. The Heart's Desire was given to mortals so they might better understand each other and then there's the Crocodile's Tear . . .' he glanced over at Tariq's mum before continuing, '. . . which gave power over the beasts and more. Much, much more.'

'Like shape-changing?'

Mum smirked and suddenly ruffled his hair. 'I told you our son was a bright boy. Inherited my brains.'

Dad laughed. 'Yeah, but he gets his good looks from me.'

Tariq jumped up. 'The Crocodile's Tear – it's here?'

He'd been right!

'I knew it would be! You have to show me!'

Mum looked at him intently. 'And how did you know?'

Tariq forced himself to calm down but it was practically impossible. 'Would you believe a tiger told me?'

They'd been celebrating at a garden party thrown by Councillor Lupus, Artos's dad. The tiger had been in a cage and spoken to him.

Dad nodded. 'I would. You were always destined to be a powerful seer. You're in the right place, son. In Xibalba you'll be taught to achieve your full potential. Far beyond anything you could imagine.' He stared at the glowing stone. 'We have to tell Imix. She'll know what to do.'

'But, Dad, what about the Crocodile's Tear? It . . . I'm here because it summoned me.'

'It summoned all of us – those of us still willing to listen to the call of the wild.' Mum suddenly hugged Tariq. She squeezed him tightly even as she laughed. 'My clever, clever boy!'

Dad wrapped his arms round both of them. 'This is where you belong, son.'

He'd missed this. Tariq loved Nani more than anything, but he'd longed for this moment for *years*.

The World's Egg glowed brighter, swelling with light along with his happiness.

Everything was perfect.

CHAPTER 12

ARTOS

'I feel terrible,' declared Artos as he leaned over the side of the boat and splashed water over his face, hoping to quell the churning of his guts. 'Maybe it's something I ate.'

'You didn't take any of those pills to settle your stomach?' asked Livia as she sat at the prow, trailing her fingers through the water.

'I used them all up the first week at sea.'

He closed his eyes, trying to ignore the bobbing

and rocking. Submerged rocks were scattered across the entire width of the river, creating rapids that shoved the boat violently downstream.

The boatman laughed at his misery. 'It'll calm down. Just hang on to your stomach a little while longer.'

'Great,' Artos groaned. He just wanted to get back on to dry land. 'When are we setting up camp? It'll be night soon.'

'A bit further,' said the boatman. 'Need to watch out for snakes. Maybe better to sleep on the boat?'

'No thanks. I'll risk it with the snakes.'

Insects darted around his ears buzzing noisily. He glanced over at Livia. There she sat, her notebook on her lap and pen in hand. Entirely happy. Couldn't she be just a little miserable? It would make him feel a bit better.

'It's beautiful, isn't it?' Livia sighed. 'I could stay here forever.'

'What? I thought you wanted to become head of the Guild of Artificers?'

Livia's eyes were wide with excitement. 'But there's so much to discover here, Artos! Plants like nowhere else in the world! Did you see that butterfly earlier? The one with the purple and silver wings? It followed us for ages!'

'I was too busy feeding the fishes.'

'Feeding the fishes? But . . . Oh. I see. That was a euphemism for being sick, wasn't it?'

'You tell me. You're the clever one.'

His attention was caught by a sudden burst of colour amongst the trees.

It was a macaw, flapping its red and gold wings as it settled on a branch. It looked at him and nodded. Hadn't there been a macaw at Lord Marius's mansion that first night?

'He's back,' said Artos, pointing at the bird.

Livia frowned as she watched the bird. 'It's been trailing the river all day.'

'Following us?' asked Artos. 'Why?'

'Hmm. We're in a strange land – there'll be plenty of things we don't understand and need to watch out for.' Livia shuffled alongside him and pointed at something swimming ahead. 'Like those.'

'It's an eel. We've plenty of them in the rivers back home.'

'Not like these. They're electric eels; we've one in the city aquarium. Even the big beasts stay away from it. It produces an energy that disables its victims, causing them to lose control of their bodies. Stuns, even kills them.' She peered at it wistfully. 'Electricity. That's worth researching.'

Artos instead gazed out at the mangrove trees that lined the river with their exposed roots spreading like straws into the water. Bats flitted within the dense canopies, doing their best to control the mosquito population. A jaguar roared from somewhere far away. The jungle seemed endless.

'For how long, though?' he muttered.

'What did you say?' asked Livia, closing her book and tucking it away. Into Right-Hand-Side Pocket Six probably.

'Just talking to myself. How long will Dandaka be like this, Livia? We've brought the Harvester. These trees? They'll be tables and chairs for the rich soon enough. This jungle will be gone, and all those butterflies and flowers that live here right now? They'll be gone too.'

Livia stared at him, horrified.

'We'll make rules. Laws to protect the environment,' she said weakly.

'Who'll make these laws? The likes of Lord Marius? I know how it works, Livia. We're bringing civilisation, and all this jungle, all this raw beauty, all this mystery, that's just getting in the way. So make the most of it while you can.'

'But how can we stop it? How can we save Dandaka?'

'By leaving and never coming back.'

Artos pondered. How could she not have realised earlier? Sometimes engineers got so caught up in their designs and all their cleverness they never really looked further than the end of their rulers. And he'd seen the way Febian had been looking at the Harvester. To be honest, he'd had the same thought: that Livia had built a deadly weapon. The days of meeting your enemy face to face, with nothing but skill and courage between you, were numbered. Soon all you would need to do is turn a handle. You couldn't control progress.

'But it's too late. There's too much money to be made.'

He hadn't noticed but they'd passed the rapids. The river was wider here, a hundred metres across at least, and as smooth as glass. Artos settled back on his bench with a deep sigh. Maybe he could get some sleep on the boat before they reached the drop-off point in the morning? Then it was all on foot. He couldn't wait.

Livia nudged him. 'Look over there, Artos.'

'Do I have to?'

'Yes, you really do,' she said urgently.

He detected tension, even fear, in her voice, so when he got up he also slipped his sword from its scabbard. 'What am I looking at?'

Livia, kneeling at the prow, pointed dead ahead. 'That.'

Artos squinted. The full moon cast an eerie ghost light over the polished black surface of the river. It was flat except for . . . 'A log?'

It must have come from upstream somewhere, slowly drifting down. It was huge. Artos reckoned the wood could have completely refurnished every single table and chair in his parents' townhouse with enough left over for the main doors. Livia saw the glorious wonder of the jungle; Artos, thanks to his upbringing, saw a vast money-making machine. Trees like that one would be just the beginning. Soon it would be—

'It blinked. The log blinked,' he said, tightening his grip on his sword. He turned to the boatman. 'We need to get to shore!'

The boatman didn't ask why. He cranked up the engine and spun the wheel to starboard. The boat shook as the engine went into overdrive. The propeller axle whined as it churned the water hard.

The crocodile changed direction with a flick of its tail. It was coming after them.

'Get us to shore right now!' Artos yelled as he ran to the back of the boat. He grabbed hold of a long pole the boatman had used earlier to shove the boat off the jetty. It was solid wood with a thick iron spike at the end. Its length would serve him better than his sword.

He stood at the aft, pole raised, eyes on the target, while the engine began screaming as the boatman pushed it beyond its limits.

The crocodile was getting closer. It raised its

head out of the water and parted its jaws. A pair of tiny yellow eyes glowed with vicious anger. This was its kingdom and they were intruders.

Timing was everything. Artos dropped his sword to hold the pole with both hands, ready to launch it like a harpoon. He had one shot and the crocodile's skin was knobbly, thick and hard. Even with his full strength, the spike wouldn't penetrate it. He had to aim at its weak spot, the open mouth. But this would only open fully at the moment of attack, when it was about to bite. And one bite would be enough. There would be no second chances.

'How are we doing?' he shouted.

'Twenty metres to shore!' Livia yelled back.

Twenty? They only needed a few more seconds and they'd be on land.

The crocodile knew it too. With one final powerful shove from its muscular tail it surged forward, opening its mouth wide enough to swallow the back half of the boat.

Artos screamed out in rage and hurled the pole with all his might.

CHAPTER 13
ARTOS

The pole went in straight and true between the crocodile's massive jaws. It pierced the side of its mouth, knocking out a few teeth. The great reptile snapped its jaws shut, smashing the rear of the boat into splinters. It would have swallowed Artos whole if he hadn't leapt out.

The crocodile swung its head from side to side, lifting the boat out of the water and ripping at its flimsy hull with deadly claws.

'This way!' yelled Livia as Artos surfaced, spluttering. She was at the riverbank, between the mangrove roots, holding out her hand for him.

Coughing, half sinking into the mud, Artos waded towards her. The boatman was already climbing out and running off into the forest, screaming. He'd lost his sword. He hadn't even had a chance to swing it in real battle and now it was sunk in the mud! But right now they had bigger problems.

'Don't wait for me!' he shouted.

Livia looked back and their eyes met. He saw her hesitate, torn between helping her friend and listening to him.

They both had their talents, and he'd never think to help her with her calculations; he'd get it all wrong. He didn't want her in the way. It was that simple. It wasn't about being heroic but being practical. Artos glowered and hissed through his gritted teeth. 'This is my fight.'

She nodded once and worked her way ahead of him.

The crocodile, gripping the middle of the boat

between its jaws, smashed both its arms hard either side, demolishing the vessel once and for all. The engine hissed angrily as it sank into the waters, steam briefly marking its final resting spot.

They needed to get away while the crocodile was distracted by the remains of the boat. Livia led, wriggling between the roots, trying to get out of the swampy mud at the edge of the water, desperate for some solid land to run on.

The crocodile made a strange blood-chilling cry, half-hiss and half-roar. It splashed back down into the water as it spat out shards of wood and bites of metal. It turned its colossal head and found them. It wasn't finished.

Using its powerful stubby legs it ran towards them. The roots snapped like twigs under its irresistible charge.

'What is it about this thing?' Artos snarled. He pulled out his dagger. The backup weapon felt ridiculously puny against the scaly behemoth.

The crocodile tore the trees apart with the same ease it had demolished the boat. Mangrove trees crashed down around the beast, barely halting its progress and only making it more berserk.

Knee-deep in mud, trapped under a labyrinth of tree roots, insects buzzing all around him and facing a monster with teeth longer than his hand, Artos didn't feel scared. He'd gone past fear so quickly he hadn't even noticed. His breath hissed between his clenched teeth and he gripped his dagger so tightly his arm shook.

One good thrust, that's all I ask for. Just one good hit before . . . whatever follows.

That was it for him. Death might be only seconds away, but that was the future and he was totally in the here and now. Each heartbeat was a lifetime. Each breath an eternity of existence.

The crocodile slowed its charge to try and catch him but the roots became more of a problem. It was still breaking them, but without the momentum of the charge it didn't have the freedom of full movement. It wasn't much but Artos needed to use any and every advantage.

He hurled himself to the left and ran the dagger along the crocodile's snout, but the blade barely cut through the knobbly scales. Its ancient skin was tougher than the best armour of the Silver Guard. It didn't do anything but annoy it like a biting insect, harmless but irritating.

More roots snapped. More trees swayed. There was thunderous crashing as one fell, snapping branches and thrashing the heavy clumps of leaves.

He had to be careful or he'd get trapped under a trunk . . .

Trapped under a trunk? Now that was an idea. One trunk wouldn't be enough, but what about four or five? The perfect cage, even for a monster like this.

Artos grinned at the beast and beckoned it closer. 'Is that the best you've got? I'm right here. Come and get me!' If the roots were causing it problems, good. He was planning on using them to cause many more.

But the crocodile was old and canny. It paused, swishing its tail back and forth, its body quivering as it anticipated a devastating charge.

Artos picked up a clod of mud and threw it in the monster's face. 'I'm getting bored.'

Did it understand him? It was sneering, or maybe that's just the way a crocodile smiled.

There was one brief moment when it was utterly still. All its power had collected and was held . . . then exploded.

Artos gasped as it tore towards him, ripping up the roots as it charged. Which was *exactly* what he wanted.

Their roots decimated, the trees tumbled down, each pulling down another until the thunder of trees falling filled Artos's ears and shook his body. He turned and crawled, hand over hand, through the cage of roots, even as he felt the stinking breath of the crocodile at his back. Any moment now those jaws would snap shut round his legs and . . .

'Artos!' screamed Livia from ahead, somewhere in the darkness.

More thrashing, more trees crashing.

'Artos!'

He was panting hard, trembling all the way through. The crocodile was right behind him!

Then the trees collapsed. They had been shaking

out of the ground and now fell like an avalanche on their gigantic scaled tormentor.

'Artos!'

Using his powerful shoulders, Artos forced his way out. His hands felt solid ground. Slick but solid. He dug his fingers into the wet soil and pulled himself free.

The trees shook behind him, the leaves rustling angrily as a frustrating hiss rose from the crocodile, imprisoned within its cage of tree trunks.

Trembling, Artos got to his feet and looked back.

There had to be six trees lying on top of the crocodile. Every now and then they would shake, and through the wreckage peered out a pair of shiny yellow eyes.

Livia stumbled beside him, staring at the cage. 'As . . . as constructions go I'd give that an "A" for effort.'

The creak of the branch overhead made Artos turn. If he hadn't been so exhausted, he would have been ready, but this was one attack too many. A muscular furred shape dropped out of the trees and slammed into the ground behind him. Artos raised his dagger but not quickly enough. A thick forearm knocked the blade out of his grip and sent it spinning away into the darkness, lost.

Then the silver gorilla, the very one he'd fought last night back in New Ethrial, raised itself on to its legs, towering over him and Livia, beating its chest in challenge.

Artos glared at it bitterly. 'Now that's just not—'

Then it swung its huge fist into Artos's jaw and he flew off into unconsciousness.

CHAPTER 14
TARIQ

Tariq knew the difference between dreams and visions. Both came while he slept, but he had a greater awareness in his visions – they were experiences he could, partially at least, explore.

Such as he was doing now.

He was back in Ethrial, the city of a thousand canals. It was bathed in glorious sunlight, the sky a brilliant blue, not a cloud in the sky. The wind was warm, tinged with sea salt. Birds swooped

123

between the towers and grand palaces. But all the people were gone.

Tariq stopped to watch a tiger lap water from a fountain. The majestic beast wore a velvet cap over one ear. It didn't seem odd, but Tariq couldn't understand it.

Sheep baaed as they strolled along the street, with their aprons dragging in the dirt. A monkey sat on a table in a shop doorway, helping itself to a pile of fruit. He spotted Tariq and held out an apple. 'Help yourself, Tariq.'

Tariq took the apple, polished it on his sleeve and bit deep. Delicious. He nodded at the monkey. 'Thanks.'

'Anything for the saviour of Ethrial. Shame how it all turned out.'

Geese waddled past, honking loudly. One had a lace bonnet on its head, and another wore a green silk cape.

Tariq finished the apple. 'What happened?'

The monkey paused as it looked up at him. 'You. Sometimes it's better not to help.'

'I'm just trying to make the world a better place,' he replied.

The monkey shrugged and tossed his own apple core into the canal. 'So is she.'

The greenish water rippled as something huge swam in the depths. Knobbly dark scales broke the surface and Tariq stared as the beast continued leisurely on in its way.

The monkey put on a hat and swung up on to the shop roof. It dangled off the ledge with one hand and looked back at him. 'Take care of yourself, Tariq.'

*

The sun was still rising but Xibalba was already busy. Tariq was down by the lake, helping haul in the nets with Foriz. Small fires dotted the lakeshore and fish were already cooking on skewers. The smell of baking bread drifted in the still cold air, and he could hear steady rhythmic thudding as grain was pounded in big stone mortars.

He'd been up an hour already, wading into the lake to watch the dawn mist lift off its mirror-flat surface as the first of the canoes went out.

What did that vision mean? What was it trying to tell him? Why had Ethrial been ruled by animals?

He'd had fragments of the same vision as they'd been crossing the ocean but never so clear and complete till now. Maybe he should talk it through with his parents. There might be a seer in Xibalba who could explain it to him.

Tariq shook the water out of his ears as he and Foriz gathered their reward, a fish skewer each dipped in spice. The best breakfast ever.

Foriz lay back with her hands behind her head. 'I've sent word to the smugglers; some of the locals here trade with them. With any luck I'll be sailing off back to civilisation within the week.'

'Oh. Why?'

She frowned. 'What do you mean "why"? I'm not spending my life living in the jungle. There are fortunes to be made. Maybe not in Ethrial, but I could start again somewhere like Kilim. Always wanted to visit there. They say all you have to do is dig a metre deep to find sapphires. Everyone lives like a queen.'

'Is that the only thing that makes you happy? Money?'

'Maybe, maybe not. But I'd rather be rich and unhappy than poor and unhappy.' She sighed. 'But . . . I'm going to do things differently. I'm not leaving without taking a few others with me.'

'What do you mean? People here? They're happy in Xibalba. I'm happy in Xibalba.'

She squinted against the morning sunlight as she looked at him. 'Of course you are. You're back with your family. I've been a slave these last few months. No one deserves that life. Night after night I heard the people around me talking about their homes, the families they'd left behind. You think I'm a criminal, Tariq. Yes, I am, and I'm proud of it. Some laws need to be broken if there's to be any justice in the world.'

He'd never heard her talk like this. There was none of her old contempt for those weaker than herself.

'Shipping people may be the law, but it's a worse

crime than anything I ever did. It's got to stop. I'll find a way to smuggle people back home.'

Tariq was puzzled. 'But they have no money. Where's the profit?'

Foriz turned slowly, grinning. 'Oh, I'll find a way, trust me. I'll make Ethrial pay. Those greedy councillors making their profits from shipping innocent people to the ends of the earth. Who knows, Tariq. You might even want to help.'

'I'm no criminal,' he replied.

Foriz's green eyes glinted with more than sunlight. 'No, you're a rebel, which is worse. You're just searching for your cause.'

A horn sounded.

People turned their attention towards the deep, long call.

'What's up?' Tariq asked the boy beside him.

'Hunting party's back,' he said. 'Let's see what they've caught. You can get bored of fish!'

The horn sounded again and people stopped working and headed towards it.

The boy frowned. 'Sounds like they've caught more than they bargained for. Come on!'

There was a shout from the centre of the crowd, a girl's voice raised in anger. '*Will you take your hands off me? And give me back my notebook!*'

Foriz groaned. 'I recognise that voice . . .'

And so did Tariq. 'Come on.' He hurried towards the crowd as it gathered in the square.

'Livia? What are you doing here?' Tariq pushed his way through the crowd towards his friends. Both Artos and Livia had their hands tied behind their backs and were filthy with mud, their clothes torn and both covered in scratches. Artos was sporting a massive black eye.

'Looking for you,' said Artos, but his attention was drawn to Foriz. 'Her not so much.'

Foriz stood there, arms folded across her chest. 'Thought you'd have been eaten by a tiger by now. But I'm used to being disappointed.'

Livia rolled her eyes, then she came up to Tariq and looked him over. 'Glad you're OK.'

Tariq grinned. They were back together; that was all that mattered. 'Artos? What happened to your face?'

Artos squinted at him through a huge black eye and indicated the gorilla. 'Him.'

Mum gestured at Livia and Artos. 'Friends of yours?'

'They're good people, Mum,' said Tariq.

Mum nodded at one of the party, a woman with parrot feathers in her hair. 'Cut them free.'

Moments later they were loose of their vine bonds. Tariq hugged them both. 'There's so much I have to show you. This place is unbelievable!'

Livia rubbed her glasses and then took in the view. 'So this is Xibalba? It must be thousands of years old. Early Water Dynasty.'

Tariq laughed. What else should he have expected from Livia? 'It's where the seers learnt their magic. And it's ruled by Imix.'

She shook her head. 'Impossible. Imix was around ten centuries ago. Even us elves don't live that long and she was, according to the stories, a korr like Artos.'

'There's power here,' said Tariq. 'Can't you feel it?'

Artos rubbed his wrists. 'We're not seers like you.'

'They took my tool kit,' complained Livia. 'Just threw it away! Now what am I going to do?'

'I'll sort something out,' said Tariq, turning to Mum. 'Can they stay with us? For the time being?'

'That'll be up to Imix,' she replied. 'They're not one of us, Tariq. They don't belong here.'

'I'm happy to leave any time,' said Artos. 'I've seen enough. We need to get some supplies together and have someone point us in the right direction. You'll need to pack, Tariq.' He turned his attention to Foriz. 'I suppose you can come if you want.'

Foriz laughed humourlessly. 'Oh? And be put in chains again? No thanks. I have my own arrangements.'

Livia gave Tariq another tighter hug. 'We found you; that's all that matters.'

They wanted to take him back! Of course they did. But . . . 'I'm not leaving Xibalba. Not yet.'

Livia frowned. 'What do you mean "not yet"?'

'There's so much here for me to learn, Livia. This is how you feel when you're at the Guild. It's where all the knowledge is, all the teachers are. I have to stay and learn everything. Look around you, have you ever seen so many seers in one place?'

'Learn what?' asked Artos.

Where to begin? Just as Xibalba merged with the jungle, so mortals and beasts mingled with ease, all equal and free. He'd watched a seer having a conversation with a jaguar while it was sitting on a bough, its tail swishing lazily as it had growled, making the seer laugh. Who knew jaguars had a sense of humour! How amazing it would be to be able to talk, actually talk, with animals. He remembered that caged tiger back in Ethrial and how stunned he'd been when it had said his name. But the seers here were having proper conversations with wild animals. Then there were the shape-changers. Only a handful of seers could do it, switching between animal and mortal forms with the ease of swapping clothes. Some struggled, that was true – he saw their pain as their bodies morphed in stages, limbs distorting, skulls melding from one form to another and bare skin suddenly growing fur. Others would encourage them, chanting and performing ritual dances to help the transformation.

'I thought we were here to find the Crocodile's Tear and go home,' said Artos. 'That was the plan.'

'It still is, sort of,' said Tariq. 'But I've been struggling alone with my powers, Artos.'

Artos frowned. 'Not alone.'

'You know what I mean. You've got the Silver Guard. Livia's got the Guild. You have teachers, mentors, traditions to guide you. I haven't had any of that till now. If I'm to help, to truly make use of my powers, then I need to reach my full potential. Surely you can see that?'

How could he leave without learning to shape-change? What animal might he become? Some big cat like Mum or a bird of prey like Dad? To have the power of a jaguar or to be able to soar the endless sky as an eagle? It was impossible to decide.

Tariq had asked his parents about their own transformations last night, but Dad had merely said, 'Imix will teach you, like she taught us.'

Imix! It all came back to her. But where was she?

People shouted from the shore. The horn sounded once more and a huge cheer rose from the crowd.

'What's going on?' Tariq asked.

Mum put her arm across his shoulders. 'Come and see.'

She led them down to the water. The sun was over the treetops now and the lake sparkled. Birds circled over the fishing boats, but everyone had stopped what they were doing, and they were watching as something came closer.

It was half submerged, moving with powerful steady strokes of its immense scaly tail.

It was the monster crocodile and it was heading towards the shore.

Tariq's heart pounded as he started backing away. He'd seen what the great beast was capable of. They needed to run before it attacked them.

But no one else seemed scared. They seemed *thrilled*.

Tariq trembled. Not with fear, not quite, but with anticipation.

Mum and Dad threw up their arms and roared in excitement along with the others. Tariq felt the wave of power building, felt it deep in his soul. All these seers together, amplifying their innate powers, creating a zone of raw energy. Tariq couldn't hold back and howled.

The crocodile slowed down as it reached land. Some people fell on their knees in awe as it clawed its way up the muddy slope, its scaly skin glistening in the morning sunlight.

Tariq's heart beat harder, as if the blood in his body was surging with new energy. Energy radiating from the crocodile.

The beast was on land now and he saw that it was colossal, easily twenty metres long and as broad as an oak tree. The skin was pitted, marked with ancient scars from a lifetime of battle, and as it flexed its jaws he shivered at the length of its jagged teeth. It ran a long tongue over its snout, then shook itself.

And began shrinking. The tail receded into the body. The scales sank into the skin, turning bare and brown. The long snout pulled into its face and the stubby limbs thinned and lengthened, its claws turning into hands with five fingers.

People pushed closer, forcing Tariq, Livia and Artos to the front.

'I don't believe it,' whispered Livia.

The crocodile twisted its torso, loosening itself up. It rose up on a pair of short legs. The scales were all but gone as it drew its hand over its face and then squeezed out its thick waist-length white hair.

The crocodile was gone and a korrish woman, old yet straight-backed and thick-set, stood in its place. Her body was covered in tattoos and she wore a tunic of reptile skin while an ornate obsidian necklace hung round her neck. Her hair was plaited and decorated with coloured stone rings. Then she walked right towards Tariq. He stood there, paralysed, trapped in the glow of the old woman's power.

He fell to his knees. He couldn't stop himself.

The old woman put her hand on his shoulder. 'Get up, Tariq. I've heard so much about you.'

He shook his head. He couldn't even speak.

'Get up, my child,' she urged, helping him by taking his arm.

He needed her strength – all his had vanished.

Then, face to face, she smiled. 'I'm Imix.'

CHAPTER 15
LIVIA

She'd seen a crocodile transform into an old woman. Seen it. There'd been fifty other witnesses. But she could not believe it.

No, she could believe it. Livia just couldn't understand it. Yet.

Transformations were a fundamental part of nature. A seed became a tree. A caterpillar changed into a butterfly. They were so familiar Livia had stopped marvelling at them, forgetting how wondrous it all was. But there was a huge difference. A butterfly couldn't change back. A tree could not shrink back into the soil and return to being a seed. One species could not change into another.

Imix let them stay together in Tariq's parents' house. It was a large stone building with tree roots growing through the walls, one roof missing but covered by woven branches and the walls decorated with weathered carvings. Definitely Early Water Dynasty, back in the long-ago age when the lands were ruled by seers or at least what they were before they were called seers. Priest kings and queens was a better translation.

Was this the beginning of a new kingdom? Imix was adored here, almost worshipped. She acted as if she was just one of them, but she wasn't. Could she be the legendary Imix? Everyone knew her stories, her adventures, about how she'd stolen the spiritstones and hidden them across the world to prevent them being misused for evil. That was one story. The other was she'd stolen them for herself, to set herself up as a tyrant across all the kingdoms of the world, and how a band of adventurers had hunted and defeated her at the cost of their own lives. Which tale was true? One or the other? Neither . . . or both?

A shadow fell over Livia from the doorway.

'Am I disturbing you?' asked Imix. She wore a plain tunic of spun nettles, dyed with rich earthy colours of ochre and red. Along with her necklace she wore beaded bracelets and an ornate feathered headdress that wasn't quite a crown but close. A cloak made of reptile skins – lizard, snake, crocodile – hung from her shoulders. She was as wild and beautiful as a jungle animal, full of quiet power. And she knew it. Her smile was condescending. She asked permission but it never crossed her mind she might be refused. It was tyranny disguised with good manners.

'What if I said I was busy?' replied Livia.

Imix looked around the room. 'Busy doing what?' Then she came in and, spreading out her cloak, sat opposite Livia, wincing as she crossed her legs. 'These knees aren't as supple as they used to be.'

'I can imagine. Still, you're pretty active for someone who's a thousand years old. What's your secret?'

'Eating well and lots of fresh air.' Imix breathed deeply. 'Ah, refreshed for another fifty years at least.'

Imix rested her chin on her fist and narrowed her gaze. In the semi-darkness of the stone chamber, those soft brown eyes seemed reptilian yellow. She might be human now but the crocodile was lurking just under the skin. 'You're the clever one, aren't you?'

'Clever?' asked Livia. Coming from anyone else it would have been a compliment. From Imix it seemed a warning. 'What makes you think that?'

'Oh, a little bird told me,' said Imix.

'That bird wouldn't be a red and gold macaw, would it?' Livia replied. She'd had her suspicions the bird had been doing more than just idly following them, and judging by the twitch in Imix's smile she was right. The macaw was working for Imix. Livia needed to warn her that spying wasn't appreciated. 'It would be a shame if that beautiful bird should end up in a cage. I know Artos's father would love one for his zoo.'

Imix's eyes narrowed. 'Clever indeed. You want answers, the real ones. Such cleverness is rare. Most people just believe what they're told. Others aren't even aware there are mysteries that need solving. They're too focused on what they already believe in, don't want that knowledge to be disturbed in any way. Closed minds are safe minds.' Then she reached into her cloak and drew out Livia's notebook. 'You dropped this back in the jungle.'

Livia held out her hand. 'Dropped it? Your warriors took it from me!'

Imix licked her thumb and looked through the pages. 'Such wonderful drawings. That butterfly looks ready to flutter right off the page. You're quite an artist. Really capture the nature of your subject.' Imix handed the notebook over, then turned suddenly. 'Ah, your companions.'

She sprang to her feet with a nimbleness Livia would have found hard to match, just as Tariq and Artos pulled back the curtain.

Tariq looked surprised. Artos looked annoyed.

'L-Lady Imix,' stammered Tariq. He bowed. 'We're honoured by your presence.'

Imix laughed. 'Please, less formality, Tariq. We're not in Ethrial, with its lords and ladies. This is Xibalba. We're all equals here. Just Imix.'

Artos scoffed but Tariq didn't notice. But Imix did. She drew her finger along a cut on her cheek. Right where Artos had thrown the pole in the battle against the monster crocodile.

Livia looked past them. 'Where's Foriz?'

Artos shrugged. 'Saw her take a canoe. She's probably paddled off to find some smugglers. Good riddance if you ask me.'

'By herself? The jungle's full of wild animals!' said Livia, before wincing. She turned to Imix. 'No offence.'

Imix smirked. 'None taken, but you're right. The jungle's a dangerous place.'

'I'd feel more worried about any beasts unfortunate to bump into Foriz than the other way round,' continued Artos. 'Foriz can take care of herself.'

142

Maybe Artos had a point. Still, Livia didn't like the idea of Foriz going off, but it's not as if she could have stopped her. Foriz only cared about Foriz.

Imix looked at each of them and bowed. 'The saviours of Ethrial. I heard the stories of what you did from the smugglers and pirates who ply their trade across the ocean. They were full of a grand tale, of how you prevented the city from being destroyed by a tidal wave. A tidal wave summoned by the World's Egg. May I see it?'

Tariq nodded and fumbled with his satchel. Livia wanted to stop him, but he was all too eager to show off the Egg and a moment later he had handed it over.

Imix raised it towards the sunlight streaming through the cracked wall. 'Ah, just as I remember it. So it ended up in Ethrial? Amongst the engineers? Truly each spiritstone has many legends of their own. Here, you take care of it.'

Tariq shook his head. 'No. I think you should—'

Livia reached over and plucked the Egg from Imix's hand, handing it back to Tariq, who took it almost reluctantly. 'Thank you and yes, we shall take very good care of it.'

Imix flashed a smile that was anything but friendly. Then she shrugged. 'You asked me what my secret was, Livia. Now that all three of you are here, I want to show you something.'

'Show us what?' asked Artos.

Imix looked surprised. 'Why, what else? The Crocodile's Tear.'

CHAPTER 16
ARTOS

The Crocodile's Tear. They were finally going to see it.

Artos glanced at the other two, wondering if they were as eager as him. Livia looked anxious. What had Imix said to her before they'd arrived? He didn't trust her.

But Tariq clearly did. He walked along as if caught in a dream, a blissful, wonderful dream.

Artos knew the feeling. He'd felt like that the

first day he'd joined the Silver Guard. He'd walked proudly through the main gates of the Guardhouse in his suit of armour, unaware of the scowls and surly looks coming from the other guards who were disgusted that a korr should be joining their esteemed elven band of warriors.

He hoped Tariq wasn't in for the same rude awakening.

He needed to keep an eye on Imix. In case the others had forgotten, she had led the attack on New Ethrial, the town he'd sworn to protect. It was a miracle no one had been killed, but plenty had been badly injured and half the town demolished.

Imix had to pay for the harm she'd done. There were rules, laws.

But it seemed Imix and Xibalba had laws of their own. The law of the jungle, and it was red in tooth and claw. He needed to be careful; they all did.

'This is the Royal Road,' said Imix. 'You can see that once it would have been far grander, but the jungle takes everything in the end.' She stopped along the crumbled path that led from the city to the limestone hills beyond and pointed at a fallen statue that was all but covered in vines. 'There. One of the ancient priest queens.'

Artos peeled back some of the foliage, revealing a face than was both mortal and feline. 'Who was she?'

Imix shrugged. 'Much of the language of that age is gone. I've been able to decipher some of the writing, but much of it is too deteriorated to read or too obscure to translate. We are peering far into the darkness of the past with only the feeblest light to help us. Still, it was here I learnt the mystery of shape-changing.'

'With the help of the Crocodile's Tear?' asked Tariq eagerly.

Imix nodded, then she pointed ahead. 'Those are the steps to the Temple of Beasts.'

The midday sun beat down as they reached the temple steps and began to climb. The steps, worn smooth by the ages, were mere dents in the cliff face now, and Artos found the view dizzying. The cliff was covered in huge carvings from the time when the elements, beasts and mortals had all lived side by side. There were elementals that had the shape of men and women, fiery lords and ladies of trees and earth, and countless beastfolk. Lions on two legs, eagle-headed mortals, and those with the bodies of women but great wings spreading from their shoulders. Did these figures ever really exist or were they the fantasy of the ancient sculptors?

'Look at the view,' said Tariq.

Artos saw Livia grit her teeth. So she was scared of heights. Now she understood the fear that filled his heart whenever he got on the boat! But she turned and looked at the view.

It was worth it. The lake shimmered like a vast mirror surrounded by dense jungle, while the river meandered its way towards the sea, disappearing swiftly out of view. The city of Xibalba clung to the lakeshore, a mixture of ancient stone temples and palaces and newly built wooden huts. The city square was crowded with people trading with each other from dozens of stalls. Wild animals mingled freely.

Most of the city was still lost in the deep jungle. What they'd cleared was just a small area along the lake. The original city stretched for kilometres. There were hills covered in vegetation that had temples beneath them, their ancient mysteries hidden for centuries.

Xibalba was vast, a rival to New Ethrial. As time went on, Artos imagined Xibalba would expand northwards, following the river, and New Ethrial would grow south, also following the river. Sooner or later they'd crash into each other.

Could the two communities live in peace, or was there trouble ahead?

'Other cities,' said Imix, pointing to the hills that dotted the panorama. 'Xibalba was the capital of what was once a vast empire. There are remains of roads heading off in all directions and we've started clearing a few of the nearby sites. None are as grand as Xibalba but they're wonderful nevertheless.' She looked towards Livia. 'Years of forgotten history, an entire civilisation, just waiting to be rediscovered.'

'There must be a dozen cities at least,' said Livia.

Imix nodded. 'It would take several hundred years to study them all, but what's that to an elf, eh?'

Of all the mortals, the elves lived the longest. Councillor Theodora was almost a thousand and had lived in Ethrial when it had just been a cluster of villages in a swamp. And, unlike humans, and to a lesser extent korrs, elves didn't change much once they reached adulthood. They didn't become old and feeble. They remained at their peak, physically and mentally, right till the end. It was only the last decade of an elf's life when time started catching up with them, and that was more through weariness than actual decrepitude. It was probably why elves eventually only kept the company of elves as they grew older and began outliving their human and korrish companions.

Artos turned cold at the thought. He'd never thought how, no matter what great friends they might be now, that it was just a brief moment in Livia's life. She could spend decades here and the time would mean nothing to her. She would return to Ethrial and find him and Tariq old men, their lives all but spent.

Livia polished her glasses. With all this damp heat they were always getting steamed up. 'That would be quite a task.'

Artos knew her well enough to realise she ached to be the one to do it. There was so much here: the plant life, the animals, the cities. She would never be bored, not for a hundred years. He had thought they'd be friends forever, but now he wasn't so sure.

They climbed on, and soon any fear of heights was replaced by the excitement to discover what was waiting for them. It didn't take them long to find out.

At the top of the stairs they walked on to a paved plateau. Ahead stood the temple.

The Temple of Beasts wasn't a building. It had been cut deep into the cliff face. The entrance was ten metres high and five wide, with huge panels of exquisitely carved scenes from the oldest legends and images of ancient gods, and descended from them were three beams of light inlaid with real gold and glowing in the sunlight. Each beam held within its light an image of one of the spiritstones, the gift of the gods.

The World's Egg for the elemental spirits.

The Crocodile's Tear for the beast lords.

Finally the Heart's Desire for the mortal people of humankind, elf and korr.

And in the centre of the wall was an opening guarded by statues of fire-breathing dragons.

Imix approached the entrance and went in.

Tariq followed without hesitation.

Artos paused at the entrance, unable to see anything in the darkness beyond. 'I don't like this.'

Livia peered in. 'We've come this far, haven't we?'

'Do you trust Imix? I don't.'

Livia frowned. 'She's led us to the Crocodile's Tear.'

'OK, but keep your eyes peeled for anything strange.'

'Like a crocodile that transforms into an old woman?'

Artos grimaced. None of the sunlight penetrated further than a metre in. Beyond was pure darkness. 'I've a feeling the strangeness is only beginning.'

He took a deep breath and stepped in.

CHAPTER 17
TARIQ

Imix whispered to herself and the darkness was obliterated as fire pits blazed into life.

She gazed around the vast cavern. 'The Temple of Beasts.'

Stalactites hung from the ceiling, pools of water dotted the floor and stalagmites created a forest of stone. The walls were painted with colossal images of beastfolk and the priest kings and queens. Stick-figure hunters chased herds of buffalo and fished rivers that overflowed with life. There were elves and korrs as well as humans, each sharing the bounty of the wild. Winged women flew through swirling clouds amongst flocks of birds, and stag-headed men locked antlers in tests of strength and honour.

Livia peered closely at one of the great hunting scenes. There was an outline of a hand and she spread her own over it. 'Mortal but with claws.'

'This is far more ancient than Xibalba,' said Tariq.

'It's from when the world was new,' replied Imix. 'This is from the mythic age, a golden age. Hundreds on hundreds of centuries ago. Look here.' She pointed to a wall covered in deep grooves. 'Bears sharpened their claws here. When I found this place there were bones of bears three times the height of the tallest person, with claws longer than my hand. It matched the oldest tales I'd been taught, of how magic flowed freely across the world and everyone had the gifts of the seers. The priest rulers were selected by the population, chosen to sit on the throne, rather than simply inherit it. Chosen because they were the wisest of their kind. Imagine what it would be like if we could return to that kind of rule.'

'The Council of Ethrial is chosen along the same lines,' said Artos. 'The people best suited to guide the city.'

Imix glanced back at them. 'Are they? Or are they merely selected from the richest?'

Artos set his mouth in a thin grim line but didn't reply.

Tariq felt the power here even as they approached the next chamber. It filled him with each step – amplifying his senses and stirring dormant memories, memories that weren't his, but his ancestors'. Out of the corners of his eyes he caught glimpses of the ancient folk who'd come and worshipped and celebrated in these caves. He heard the echoes of their songs, their laughter and their cries. Half-intelligible words were whispered in his ears by the ghosts of the first of his kind. Smells wafted in the clammy cave air. Smells of incense, of food cooking, of herbs being ground on stone slabs and the smell of the animals that shared the shelter. Wolves and jaguars, and songbirds nesting in the alcoves. Bats flitted amongst the stalactites. The past was so close here in the temple. He felt if he turned the right way he could join the ancients, be transported across the countless years with only a single step.

As he entered the chamber, something glowed in the darkness, a beacon of golden light that summoned him. The light cast strange patterns on the undulating walls of the cave, giving shadows lives of their own, transforming them into animal shapes as they drew closer. The only sound was the beating of his heart.

The chamber was small, with barely enough space for the four of them. It was little more than a crack that had been eroded away by water soaking down through the rock, leaving this secret nook deep within the temple.

A stone sat within an alcove, radiating a greenish light. The surface of the stone was carved so it resembled scales. Imix reached up for it and took it out. It was the size of an apple and yet Tariq felt overwhelmed by its presence.

'The Crocodile's Tear,' said Imix, her tone one of quiet reverence. She held it out to him. 'Take out the World's Egg.'

He did. The World's Egg felt . . . more powerful than usual. It began to glow, spreading a myriad of colours across the chamber's walls.

Imix stood opposite him, cupping the Crocodile's Tear in both hands. She closed her eyes, and smiled softly.

The two stones glowed brighter, pulsing together.

A breeze entered the small chamber. The temple echoed with distant roars. Was that the sea or the roar of lions?

When Imix opened her eyes, they were the slitted yellow irises of a reptile. 'Each spiritstone holds within it unimaginable power, but it is focused and its powers only accessible by the seer within its presence. But when brought alongside another stone, its influence expands. You can use the power of the stones from a greater distance. According to the myths, when the three stones were together, their powers could be tapped by any seer anywhere across the world.'

'Is that why you stole them?' asked Livia.

Imix grimaced but nodded. 'They were at risk of being used for evil. A band of seers sought to become rulers themselves and terrorise kingdoms with the threat of tidal waves, earthquakes, war on an unimaginable scale. They invited me to join them, believing they were as wise as the priest kings of the past. They weren't. They were greedy and petty.

'I took the stones, kept the Crocodile's Tear and gave the World's Egg and the Heart's Desire to my apprentices, ordering them to take the other spiritstones far away and hide them. I hoped that would be the end of it. But I didn't understand the stones were *meant* to be kept together. That's when they are most powerful.'

'Why?' Tariq asked.

'Harmony. We are all part of the world, not distinct, separate parts. The spiritstones remind us that we are a single organism flowing together, dependent on one another, *strengthening* each other. Mortals, the beasts and the elements. I didn't realise that when I took the stones. Now I look around me and see the discord, the conflict. How mortals destroy the environment with their greed, how rivalries between kingdoms have led to mass destruction, and the way we abuse the animals that were once our kin. That needs to change, Tariq.'

Strength in unity, it all made sense. Even with these two spiritstones he felt so much stronger, more attuned to everything around him. It felt . . . amazing.

Artos stepped forward. Tariq could see the suspicion in his narrowed gaze. 'And let me guess. The person to make that change would be you?'

Imix met his gaze with a hardness of her own. 'Once the seers sat alongside kings and queens, guiding them, offering their wisdom, their powers. In service of everyone, not merely a rich elite.'

What Imix said made a lot of sense to Tariq. Seers had been outcasts for centuries now. Feared and despised because of their abilities, forced to keep them hidden. What Imix was proposing would bring them back into society, show everyone they were here to help. Didn't Artos understand that? Where would Ethrial be if it hadn't been for him, a seer, using the World's Egg? It would be under the sea.

Imix held the World's Egg beside the Crocodile's Tear. 'Think of what we could do with two stones. We could *combine* their powers. Really make a difference.'

'How?' asked Livia.

Imix frowned. 'We need to set an example. Xibalba first, and protecting Dandaka Jungle from the destruction it's being threatened with.'

Artos glared at her, his body tense and hands rolled into fists. 'Another attack? Is that what you're planning?'

Imix shook her head. 'We use the stones. Use them to make people realise what they're doing. Make them understand Dandaka should be protected, that it should be left as it is. Its wealth is not for stealing.'

Livia frowned. 'In a better world that might work. But I know the people in the Council. They want New Ethrial built and they want profits.'

'Aren't they rich enough?' asked Tariq. Then he

turned back to Imix. 'Could you really make them change their ways?'

'Yes, with your help,' said Imix. 'We will start with New Ethrial. If they can be made to see the error of their ways, then we can do the same elsewhere. It's possible now we have two stones. Their power is magnified. With only one there was little I could do. That's why I had to lead an attack, to free the animals that had been imprisoned. But with the two of us, combining the power of two spiritstones, we can remind the townsfolk of their kinship with the wild, remind them that the beasts were once their allies, all part of a single family. It's hard to put your brother in a cage.'

Everything she said made so much sense. There was a better way to live. It reminded Tariq of life in the river clan: everyone had enough and everyone shared, because the clan was one big family. Could Imix create a clan of the whole world? It was a huge idea but anything seemed possible if they had the spiritstones to help them. He'd been led to this place, answering the call of the Crocodile's Tear. The two spiritstones had been attracted to each other. He'd known he needed to find the Crocodile's Tear, to somehow use it and the World's Egg to repair the damage to the world around him. He hadn't had a plan, just a desire. But Imix? She had the plan.

Tariq addressed Imix. 'I'll do anything I can to help.'

'I'm counting on you,' said Imix. She turned to the others. 'I'm counting on all of you. We've a chance to repair centuries of damage, of turmoil. Make a fresh, better start.'

Livia huffed. 'We've got to start somewhere, I suppose.'

Artos didn't reply.

*

'I don't trust her,' said Artos as they ate their evening meal back in Xibalba. The three of them sat cross-legged on a rattan carpet with wooden bowls filled with fish stew, fresh bread and fruit.

Tariq frowned. 'Why not? She's got a vision of making a better world. You saw what Ethrial was like. All the pollution. People living squalid, miserable lives while others feasted. Something needs to change.' He looked at Livia. 'Isn't that the point of the Guild of Artificers? To build a better world?'

Livia cleaned her glasses before answering. 'What Imix wants is revolution, Tariq. The world she wants means destroying the world we have. I . . . I'm afraid of her. It's that simple. And I don't mean just because she can turn into a monster crocodile. There's something . . . cold-hearted about her. Can't you sense it?'

'No, I can't. Imix is the greatest of all seers. What's more, she is a visionary. She sees what we could be, and rather than just shrug and think it's too hard, she wants to do something about it. Look, we saved Ethrial with just one stone. With two? We could do so much good, Livia!'

Livia didn't seem convinced. 'And so much harm. This is not something we should rush blindly into. We need to carry out experiments, learn what the stones, when working together, can do.'

'Just what I'd expect an engineer to say,' said Tariq, smiling at her. 'But you're right. We need to know exactly what we're getting into. This is different from last time – we don't have a tidal wave threatening to wipe us out. I'm sure Imix will understand if we take things a little slowly.'

Artos snorted. 'She has all the time in the world, doesn't she?'

Tariq nodded. 'What's a few more years when you've lived a thousand already?'

'Where did she get all that extra time from? Korrs don't live anywhere near that length of time. It feels . . . unnatural.'

Livia looked between them. 'It is unnatural. I thought the spiritstones were all about harmony, balance. There is something extremely out of harmony with her living for so long.'

Tariq shook his head. 'We need Imix to guide us. Those centuries have given her a wisdom we can't begin to comprehend.'

'So she wants you to believe. I'm not so sure.' Artos put his bowl down with a clatter. 'In the meantime keep a close eye on the World's Egg. It's not to be let out of your sight, got it?'

'You really don't trust her, do you?'

'Who trusts a crocodile?' Artos met his gaze. 'She tried to eat me, Tariq. And don't forget she tried to do the same to you.'

Tariq stood up and brushed off the crumbs. 'I'm going to go speak with my parents. They've known Imix for a long time.'

He turned to the doorway and stopped. Just perched outside was the red and gold macaw.

He really didn't like that bird.

It snapped its beak at him and flew off.

CHAPTER 18
ARTOS

'We should have gone with him,' said Artos as he stood in the doorway, searching for Tariq. 'Tariq's been acting strangely since he got here. You must have noticed?'

Livia joined him. 'He's found his parents, his people. It's going to have an effect on him.'

'*We're* his people, Livia.'

'Does Imix really think she can change things? We can't turn back time to when we were all wearing flowers in our hair. If that time ever really existed, which I doubt.'

Artos rubbed his chin. 'I dunno. She seems to believe she can. But this is actually about Tariq. He's our friend and we're in a strange place where we don't know the rules, so we need to keep an eye out for one another. Agreed?'

'Agreed.'

They ventured out and joined the people milling around the square. With the jungle on all sides, the shadows lengthening as the sun sank towards the horizon, and the people of Xibalba wearing furs, scales and decorated in feathers, Artos felt a long way from home.

He missed the smoky air of Ethrial, the clatter of cartwheels on the cobbles and the cries of the street hawkers. Despite himself, the animal noises echoing across the jungle made his skin crawl. He was a city boy, plain and simple. There were just too many trees here and not enough buildings.

'You look lost,' said Imix, appearing from a nearby hut.

'We're looking for Tariq,' admitted Livia.

'Oh? I just saw him heading down to the lake. I think he was after some grilled fish.' Imix pointed off to the edge of the trees. 'I'll show you. I rather fancy some myself.'

'Thanks,' said Artos. 'Coming, Livia?'

Livia reluctantly joined him and the trio headed out of the city as twilight approached.

It was always gloomy under the trees, even during the day. The sun never really penetrated to the jungle floor, as if the jungle wanted to hold on to its mysteries.

Imix picked a papaya off a tree and ate as they walked. 'My people say there's a big chopping machine working its way through the jungle. Something you made, Livia?'

'It's running?' cried Livia. 'I told Febian not to touch it!'

'You can't stop progress,' said Artos. 'Isn't that what you're always saying?'

'That is not funny.' Livia grimaced. 'If he chops his foolish head off, it'll serve him right.'

'It's cutting down a lot of trees,' said Imix. Artos heard the warning in her voice.

'It's meant to,' Livia replied, who clearly didn't. 'We need to clear the jungle if we're to develop New Ethrial. Farms need a lot of land.'

'So do the animals that already live there. Did you not think to ask their permission before you stole it from them?' Imix pointed at a monkey dozing up on a bough. 'Where will he live when all the trees are gone? In a cage in some rich man's house? Have his bananas served on a silver plate?'

'You've made your point,' said Artos. 'So where's Tariq?'

They'd reached the jungle by now, away from the city and everyone.

'I'm sorry. He must have gone another way. Let's chat for a moment, then we'll head back.' Imix sat down on a tree stump. 'My legs weary quickly nowadays.'

She was exaggerating. One thing that was obvious to anyone was how tough Imix was. She walked with her head straight, no slouching or weariness, no sign of those thousand years weighing her down. Still, if she wanted a private chat, why not?

Imix peered at both of them, smiling as she shook her head. 'Everyone has an animal inside them. Or you could say that part of our nature remembers being a beast, being wild. Civilisation is new, and who knows how long it'll last? Perhaps it's just a fad.'

She pointed at Livia. 'You remind me of a mouse. Always on the lookout. Always curious. Sharp mind, quick. That's you, Livia.'

Livia looked disappointed. 'Er . . . thanks, I suppose.'

'And what beast am I?' Artos asked.

'Tenacious. Strong-willed. Perhaps too focused only on what's right in front of you. A boar.'

'A boar? I can live with that.'

Imix gazed off towards the black silhouette of the jungle beyond the boundary of the city. 'I came here thinking I'd escape from the world. There were only a handful of us back then, me and my closest students. We pieced together all the legends about Xibalba and knew it was somewhere deep in Dandaka. We took a ship, smugglers who had a hideout along the coast, and they dropped us off. I bet they thought we'd be dead within the year. I admit it was tough. But we made allies. We would never have survived without them.'

'What sort of allies?' asked Livia. 'Are there other villages here?'

'You misunderstand. I mean the beasts of Dandaka. We learnt their language. I call it the Wild Tongue. Maybe it's the language we had when we lived in harmony with nature, but we forgot it when we became . . . *civilised*. It was a jaguar who led us to Xibalba. Back then it was so overgrown you could hardly make out a single building. It took us years to clear away all the vegetation, and it's a constant battle: the jungle wants the city back. If you're not careful, you could go away for a week and come home to find a tree sprouting in your bedroom.'

'What about New Ethrial?' Artos asked. 'You know the Council wants to build a trade town here. And that's just the beginning. It sees a colony here one day. Towns along the coast, along the river.'

Imix frowned. 'That won't happen. Just because Ethrial has exhausted its own resources does not give it the right to pillage Dandaka.'

'But no one owns the jungle,' said Artos.

Imix turned to him sharply. 'No one? What about the monkey? The jaguar? The sloth? The birds and the fishes? Is not Dandaka theirs already?'

Artos lowered his head, ashamed. 'I meant people.'

Imix sighed. 'We once saw the beasts as our kin. We loved nature as we would our mother, for the natural world nourishes us. We should protect our kin, our mother. But what's happening? The things we should cherish are being ravaged, exploited – for what? Gold? What can you do with gold? It's a sickness mortals have. This obsession.

'But there is another way. One that's only possible now Tariq has brought the World's Egg. With two stones together I'm able to expand the scope of their potency. Perform more powerful magic. Tariq has learnt some of the secrets of his stone, but there are many more yet to be discovered.

I, on the other hand, have had centuries to study the Crocodile's Tear and decipher the mysteries of Xibalba.'

Artos glanced at Livia. There was something threatening about Imix, but he couldn't work out what danger they were in. Was she about to turn into a crocodile?

'I have such grand plans,' said Imix as she gazed westwards. 'But first I must deal with New Ethrial.'

Artos narrowed his eyes. 'What do you mean "deal with"?'

'Let me show you.' Imix reached into her cloak and withdrew the Crocodile's Tear. 'They say that to understand a person you need to walk in their shoes. I have another version. To understand an animal you must wear its skin.'

The spiritstone began glowing.

Imix held the stone high, so its light bathed all three of them. 'I told you everyone has a bit of animal inside them. Let's find out, shall we?'

Artos backed away. 'What do you think *snort* . . . you're *snort*—'

'Artos!' snapped Livia. 'Your *squeak* . . . your *squeak* . . . face . . .'

Artos stared at her. 'My face? What about *snort* yours? You've got *snort snort* whiskers!'

He dropped to his knees, and cramps wracked his body. It felt as if every bone was twisting out of shape!

Livia was curled up on the ground, writhing in agony, and her face began distorting as whiskers sprouted from either side of her lengthening nose and her ears . . . Elves had pointy ears but these were becoming huge and round like pancakes. And as she clutched her stomach, Artos saw a tail emerging from under her tunic and fur sprouting over her arms and legs.

Imix crouched down, peering at him with curiosity. 'I don't want to hurt you, but I need you to understand what it is to be a beast. My original plan was to launch an attack on New Ethrial, drive all its inhabitants into the sea and destroy every single building. But that was before Tariq turned up with the World's Egg. The boy has given me the key to a true poetic justice. With the Crocodile's Tear alone, I could teach transformation to only the best seers. But I felt the stone's power increase the moment Tariq presented the World's Egg. Now I can transform . . . everyone.'

Artos could hardly see for the tears of pain streaming from his eyes. Where Livia had been there was now just a small brown mouse. It darted around in circles, panicked and bewildered, squeaking with terror.

A shocking tremor went through him. He stared at his hands as they became trotters, his arms covered in black bristles. His jaw ached as a pair of curved tusks sprouted out.

'Tariq will *snort snort* . . . He will *snort* . . .'

Imix smiled. 'He will do whatever I tell him. Poor Artos, poor Livia. You really shouldn't have come here. This is the wilderness; it doesn't suit the likes of you.' She stood up slowly. 'Now, little piggy, run. Run away and hide or else I'll be having bacon for breakfast.'

The mouse squeaked at him. Artos turned round on his four trotters, struggling to balance with his new body. He was consumed by panic. What else could he do?

Imix clapped her hands. 'Run, little piggy! Run!'

And so he did. Artos the boar ran helter-skelter into the undergrowth, crashing through the foliage with a mouse darting alongside him.

CHAPTER 19
TARIQ

'Have you seen my parents?' asked Tariq. He'd looked all over for them but instead found Imix, down by the lake where it fed into one of the rivers. Bats flitted across its still surface, chasing down their evening meals.

'Probably out hunting. Twilight is the time for panthers.' She stood knee-deep in the river, hands on her hips, watching a red and gold macaw circling overhead. 'Do you trust me?'

'When someone asks that it usually means you shouldn't,' Tariq replied.

She smiled. 'Good answer. Your parents were right about you. Trust should be earnt, Tariq. I hope today I'll earn that trust. Get in. We're going for a swim.'

A swim? He wasn't going to turn that down. He kicked off his boots, slipped out of his tunic and waded in.

This was the life, the mud squelching between his toes, the current wrapping round his legs, the cold freshness of water from the mountains and the crimson sunlight shimmering on the water's surface. Fish darted past and Tariq continued further in until he was on his tiptoes. 'Where are we going?'

'Let's just explore.' And, with that, she took a deep breath and plunged in. There was barely a ripple.

Tariq filled his lungs and followed. He'd played this game before: who could hold their breath longest?

Imix was already a dozen metres ahead of him and getting further away. She seemed to put in little effort, while Tariq kicked hard and forced himself to reduce the gap. The current was stronger than he'd expected.

But what a world.

He'd never seen fish like these. Scales with dazzling stripes, fins of orange, green and bright red. The weeds sprouting between the rocks on the riverbed bloomed with wild flowers that swayed gently in the current. Tariq pushed himself into the depths to explore.

He'd hang on a little while, then come up for another breath. Imix was treading water above him; she wasn't in a rush.

Even the pebbles down here captivated him. They were semi-transparent; it was as if the riverbed was scattered with precious gems, just waiting to be picked up. Now he understood where the others had got their jewellery. The river provided everything! Just like it had when he'd been living in the river clan on the other side of the ocean.

Imix joined him as he picked a few stones. He could turn these into a necklace. There were a few fossils, perfect for a centrepiece.

He'd been down here long enough. He needed air. Tariq turned his face upwards.

Imix grabbed him.

What was she doing? She had her arms round his waist from behind and was pulling him down. What was she *doing*?

This wasn't the game he'd played back with the others from the river clan. You never pulled anyone under, *ever*. Tariq tugged to get out, but Imix dragged him deeper. Bubbles escaped from his lips as he struggled. She might have been old but she was all wiry strength, her hold unbreakable. Tariq tried to twist round but Imix tightened her grip, countering his kicks by squeezing her legs round him. Their combined weight sinking them both towards the river bottom.

Tariq's lungs burned. He fought the urge to gasp. Panic ate into his thoughts. She was going to drown him! He couldn't break free.

The surface wasn't that far away! He tried to paddle towards it, but Imix pulled him down all the harder. Wasn't she going to drown too?

Tariq couldn't hold his breath any longer.

Water poured into his open mouth. It was beyond any pain. He felt terror as well as physical agony as his lungs flooded. Desperation took over, the final fight for life, but Imix's hold was inescapable. She squeezed out the last of his air.

Why?

He felt heavy. His limbs sagged and he couldn't even keep his eyes open. The pain was fading and the panic subsided. His toes touched the bottom. Imix let him go.

Tariq sank into the mud.

*

Tariq breathed. He *breathed*.

But that . . . wasn't possible.

He opened his eyes to a peculiar world. He was underwater, but the sights around him were distorted.

How was he breathing? He saw Imix, a few metres away, watching him intently.

She'd tried to drown him!

Tariq lunged at her with a flick of his . . . tail?

He slithered through the water with inhuman

grace, as if this was his world, not the air-laden world above.

He twisted round, trying to catch himself.

No legs, no torso with arms, but a long sleek grey serpentine body, perfectly designed for life underwater.

Tariq powered along so easily now. He circled Imix, flexing his jaws with needle sharp teeth. The water tickled through his gills.

An eel! He'd turned into an eel!

He wanted to bite her, to teach her a lesson, but even as he circled closer, he felt the rage receding. She'd taught him a lesson. She'd taught him to shape-change!

To become truly one with nature.

He could shape-change!

Tariq wanted to laugh. How fast could he go? He overtook startled fish, wriggled easily between rocks and through the forest of weeds and underwater plants.

On and on he went. This was freedom! Cutting through the water, his entire body and mind were in tune, possessing a power he'd never felt as a human. It was as if this was what he was meant to be. He'd found his true self thanks to Imix.

Eventually he got tired. His body felt heavy and sluggish. Breathing was becoming hard and his muscles ached. He flicked his tail but felt only the wiggling of toes. He fought upwards with big strokes of his arms.

Tariq broke the surface and took a huge gasp.

Imix sat on the riverbank, laughing. His parents were there too. Dad waded in and offered him a hand. 'Come on, son.'

Tariq shook the water out of his ears and waded back out. 'You could have warned me!'

'It was the same for us, when Imix tested us.' Dad's smile didn't fade. 'The first transformation has to be a shock. The unconsciousness needs to fight, break down the barriers. If you'd known, it wouldn't have worked. You'd have resisted too much. You needed to give in.'

Mum smiled at him but she could see how angry he was. 'We're so proud of you, Tariq. An eel! Now that's a rare beast. You really do have river water flowing through your veins. It was Imix who said you were ready for the test. She saw the beast within you, waiting to be freed.'

'That doesn't make it any better, Mum.' He stomped out of the water, stopping only to glare at the old woman. 'I almost drowned, Imix.'

Imix slung him his boots. 'Maybe you were right not to trust me.'

*

It was night by the time Tariq made his way wearily back to Xibalba. He'd shape-changed! Imix had taken brutal measures, but they had worked, hadn't they? He'd needed to be pushed beyond his limits, and he couldn't have done that by himself.

She'd known he'd be a water creature. What had Imix done to free the beast within Dad, the eagle? Pushed him off the top of a cliff?

Where were Artos and Livia? He wanted to tell them. No, wouldn't it be better if he took them to the lake and showed them without telling them? Livia would be so shocked her glasses would crack!

Now Tariq felt he was a real seer. What next?

Talking to the animals? Or what if he could shape-change into more than one animal? Was that even possible?

Poor Livia. She would give anything to experience what it was like being another creature. How different the world was from the perspective of a creature that swam or flew. He had to tell them right now!

But as he wandered around Xibalba, his friends were nowhere to be found. They didn't need to be suspicious of Imix any more. He would tell them how great Imix was, how she was willing to share her knowledge and power. That was good, wasn't it? She was a teacher; she wanted everyone to know what she knew, to experience the world the same way as her.

There was so much to learn here, so many wonders still to be discovered. But Tariq could barely keep his eyes open. Who knew shape-changing would be so exhausting? He sank down on to the rattan carpet in the centre of the hut, cradling his head in the nook of his arm. He smelt the river, felt weeds brushing across his skin. He smiled as he closed his eyes and sank into a dream of the magical world under the water . . .

*

'Tariq? Tariq? Are you in there?'

Tariq rubbed his eyes. 'Livia? Is that you?'

He blinked. The sun was low through the doorway. He could see the dawn mist upon the lake's surface. He yawned. 'You won't believe what I did yesterday.'

But it wasn't Livia who came in; it was Foriz.

And she looked scared.

'Where have you been?' he asked. 'I was beginning to think you'd gone off and found some smugglers to take you home.'

She looked around anxiously. 'Home? Where's that? Imix isn't around, is she?'

'Is this about her?' Tariq frowned. Why was everyone so suspicious of Imix? Everything she did was to make things better. 'She's teaching me to shape-change! Can you believe it?'

Instead of looking surprised or even pleased, Foriz seemed horrified. 'Tariq, you're so wrong about her. She's dangerous. In ways you can't—'

Despite everything, he was worried. What could so frighten Foriz? He thought she was immune to fear. 'What is it, Foriz?'

She covered her face and shook with a deep, awful sob. 'I can't even believe it.'

'What did you find?' He was starting to get frightened himself.

Foriz looked up at him, face pale. 'I have to show you.'

CHAPTER 20
LIVIA

Livia woke up in a nest of leaves. She tried to rub her face but something was wrong. Her body wasn't hers. She twitched uncontrollably, her heart racing so fast she could hear the blood rushing in her ears.

She scurried to her feet, turning round to come face to face with . . .

. . . a boar. A huge bristly boar with a pair of wicked curved tusks. It lay in the shade, snoring.

Livia came closer, sniffing it. It grumbled in its sleep. It wasn't huge, she realised; she was just very small.

She was a mouse.

Imix had transformed both of them last night.

What then? Her mind was in chaos. It had been a nightmare, racing along the jungle floor, so small and the jungle so alive, so threatening. A snake had made a snatch for her; it might have got her too if the boar hadn't trampled on its head.

The boar? No, Artos.

The boar blinked, revealing a pair of pale blue eyes. It searched around until it spotted her.

'Livia? It that *snort* you?' the boar asked as it got up, swaying uncertainly until it braced itself on its four hooves.

'*Squeak*, it's *squeak* me. Now what are we *squeak* going to do?'

Artos shook his head. 'How are we speaking? How is it *snort* possible?'

'The Wild Tongue. It has to be. Imix *squeak* said it was *squeak* the language they communicate with. *Squeak squeak.*'

189

Think, Livia, think!

She might have a tail but she still had her mind.

They needed to change back. So they needed to find Tariq; he was their only hope – if he could get his hands on the Crocodile's Tear. But they were lost in the jungle now. Who knew which way Xibalba was? And Livia was a mouse! The weakest of any animal.

She had to survive. There was an urge, an almost overwhelming one, to hide down a hole.

Artos rooted around the tree. 'Imix will *snort* do this to everyone in New Ethrial.'

'And after that?'

Artos stopped. '*Snort.*'

'Exactly.' Why stop with New Ethrial?

She imagined Ethrial empty of people and overrun by animals. The Guild of Artificers filled with monkeys, mice and squirrels. Her tutor, Lady Fausta, a blinking owl perched on a roof beam. The streets filled with bears, donkeys, foxes and snakes; the city no longer filled with mortal voices but howls and shrieks and braying.

It would have been hard enough to stop Imix

normally. But now? One mouse and one hairy pig against a city of shape-changers led by the greatest seer *ever*?

'What if Tariq can't *snort* change us back?' asked Artos. 'What if we're *snort* stuck like this?'

'He has to.'

'How do you know? Imix is so powerful! Tariq's nowhere near at her level! *Oink!*'

'*Squeak!* Trust Tariq! Or do you want to spend the rest of your life rooting for *squeak* truffles?'

Artos lowered his head. 'I hate truffles.'

'There you go then. It'll *squeak* be fine. We've faced *squeak* worse situations.'

'*Oink!* No we haven't, Livia!'

Livia laughed. Or squeaked. He had a point.

She would get out of this. Things would go back to normal. Tariq would be able to undo Imix's magic. He'd already stopped a tidal wave after all! Then, when everything was back to how it should be, she'd write about her experience as a mouse. To be so small. Smaller than a stalk of grass. And how her senses had changed. As a mouse, she could smell everything differently. She could follow the flow of scents better than her vision since she was so low to the ground.

'Which way?' asked Artos.

There were so many smells it was giving her a headache. She needed to find a way of separating them and to follow the ones that were uniquely mortal.

Smoke. Cooking. The smell of food sizzling over charcoal. Only mortals cooked their food.

'That *squeak . . . squeak squeak*!'

Livia nibbled a fallen nut to calm herself. The more she stressed, the more mouse-like she became. What . . . what if the longer she remained like this, the sooner she forgot she'd ever been anything but a mouse?

She scurried off in the direction the scent of smoke was strongest. Right behind her, snorting, squealing and trampling the undergrowth, came Artos the boar.

CHAPTER 21
TARIQ

'Where are we going?' asked Tariq. 'Just tell me.'

Foriz shook her head. 'You need to see this for yourself.'

There was no point arguing with her, so he just followed. They'd turned off one of the ancient roads and were back in the gloomy world of the deep jungle again. Insects buzzed through the air, birds called from their lofty perches and the pair had to pause as a scaled lizard, three metres long, emerged from the tall grass and crossed their path, its tongue flicking and tail swishing.

The canopy rustled as monkeys swung from tree to tree on their endless search for the sweetest fruits. One paused to watch Tariq and Foriz before scratching its backside and leaping off after the rest of its brethren.

Tariq could just . . . sink into this world. He had given up on boots. He loved the feel of the damp soil between his toes and no longer bothered with his tunic. The scents of the jungle had soaked into his skin now. More and more he was merging with the natural environment. He belonged here.

There was a river running nearby. Tariq could hear the water splashing over the rocks and sense the power of the current as it fed the lake. Maybe he could just change shape and travel that way? Meet Foriz further up? Why not? Just for a little while.

'Are we following the river?' he asked.

'For a while. Why?'

'I'll meet you downstream then. A kilometre from here?'

Foriz narrowed her eyes. 'What if you . . . don't?'

'Come on, Foriz. Just for a short distance. OK, not a kilometre, just half. What's the harm in that?'

'You'll find out soon,' she replied as she set off again.

'You can't stop me. If I want to shape-change, I will.'

The look she gave him wasn't angry; it was sad. 'Nice to be special, isn't it? To have powers that others can't even imagine?'

'Whatever I do is to help people, Foriz.'

'How's shape-changing helping people? Seems to me it's all about enjoying your power. I get it. I've been there too. Who wants to be . . . average?'

'If you just spoke to Imix, you'd understand. She can make it all—'

'Shut up about Imix,' Foriz snapped. 'She's more dangerous than you can imagine. Do me a favour – walk with me the rest of the way. Be . . . you.'

'I'm always me. Who else could I be?'

But Foriz had already left. She'd disappeared into some bushes and wasn't interested in arguing.

He should just swim. That would teach her. And what did she mean about Imix being dangerous? Maybe only a seer could understand what Imix was trying to achieve.

Tariq felt too hot. A dip in the water would be just the thing. His skin was all sticky with sweat, uncomfortable, as if it didn't fit. He wanted to be sliding through the cool waters, down amongst the fishes and forests of underwater plants. To be darting through the mesmerising speckled light.

Foriz was getting further away. If he didn't go now, he'd lose her.

The river would have to wait.

'Hold on!'

The slanted early-morning light cut through the tree trunks, illuminating a patch of open ground dotted with mossy stones. Beyond was the remains of a building: nothing left but a few column stubs and walls.

Foriz was crouched low and Tariq crept up beside her. 'Is this what you wanted to show me? Another fallen-down temple?'

She tapped her finger to her lips, and pointed.

Two figures moved through the ruins. Warriors. He'd seen them at Xibalba; he couldn't remember their names but knew they were initiates – part of Imix's inner circle, like his parents. One could transform into a gorilla, the other was an otter. But what were they doing way out here? What was the big secret?

'I've been exploring the area, paddling up and downriver looking for smuggler hideouts. Didn't find them, but I found this place.' Foriz nudged him. 'Follow me.'

They crept round the outside of the ruins, behind the walls and through the long grass until they reached a pile of stones that was so covered in foliage it resembled a small hill. Foriz approached an opening just big enough to crawl in.

Tariq had a bad feeling about what was coming next. He knelt down to follow her. 'What is that stench?'

'That's your future if you're not careful. Follow me.' And, with that, Foriz slipped into the gap. With a sigh Tariq followed.

The smell grew worse. The air down here was clammy, skin-prickling. The moisture had turned the soil into sludge and the walls crawled with insects, their hard bodies clicking endlessly against each other. In the pitch black they climbed over Tariq, through his hair, even scuttling across his face. He clamped his mouth tight as mandibles prodded his lips, feeling for a way in.

Noises echoed ahead of them. Scraping. Growls, pitiful mewling. An odd savage howl. It made his skin crawl more than the insects.

Foriz slipped out of the tunnel and Tariq was quick out behind her, picking a caterpillar from his ear as he looked around.

They were deep underground. Water dripped from the porous rock overhead, the walls glowed with strange fluorescent plants and moss that partially covered ancient markings – crude outlines of beasts, mortals and those in between. And then, as his eyes became accustomed to the gloom, Tariq saw them.

Some were chained, others were in cages made of thick branches lashed with vines.

Not beasts. Not mortals.

Creatures trapped between two forms. Hybrids.

How many were there? He couldn't tell, but there had to be at least ten cages just in this cavern – different sizes but built stoutly – and there were crevasses that had wooden gates across them, lashed shut with thick vine ropes. And other caverns branched off from the space.

The two of them crept closer, Tariq following Foriz's lead.

One hybrid had the upper torso of a wolf, but its elongated face was still vaguely human, hairless and lopsided, and its lower body comprised a left canine leg while the right remained human. It hadn't fully transformed, and the creature's hips were crooked. It couldn't walk, but dragged itself around its cramped cage, sniffing at Foriz as she reached through the bars.

Tariq jerked forward. 'Foriz! Don't let it—'

The wolf creature licked her palm and let her rub its head. The other beasts turned towards them, shuffling to get closer. They recognised Foriz and knew she was a friend.

This was a side of Foriz Tariq didn't know even existed. She felt their suffering and there was a softness in her eyes, in her manner, that he'd never seen before. Was this what she had been like before her life on the streets had made her ruthless?

'Imix. She'll be able to help them,' he said.

Foriz snorted. 'Who do you think put them down here?'

Tariq couldn't believe it. 'No. She wouldn't leave them like this. She's the greatest seer of us all. She wants us to reach our full potential. She taught me how to shape-change, Foriz. She can help them change too. All the way.'

A monkey-man hybrid who'd overheard them sneered. 'Imish? I cursh the day I firssh shaw her.'

Foriz hurried to the cage. 'You can talk? What happened to you?'

The monkey man looked between them both. 'Sheers?'

'Him,' said Foriz. 'Not me.'

'You're lucky,' said the monkey man. Then he winced, rubbing his face and mewling pitifully. 'Hurtsh shpeaking. Hurtsh thinking. Not long now.'

'Not long for what?'

He gazed at Tariq, licking his lips as if trying to find the words. He screwed his forefinger against his head. 'Jush monsh . . . monshter. No more man. All gone. Shoon won't remember being anything elsh.'

Tariq backed away. What if he hadn't changed all the way? This could have been him. Trapped partway between animal and human.

So Imix was hiding her failures down here from the others. She might have tried to help them, Tariq couldn't let go of that, but even the great Imix had failed. So here they lived in cages. Soon they'd forget what they'd ever been and then what? Would she release them into the wild? They couldn't hunt the way they were; they would starve.

Had his parents known? No, they couldn't have. They would never have let Imix help him to shape-change if they'd known this could happen.

He remembered Livia's warning about testing the spiritstones. Imix had known the price of failure but that hadn't stopped her. She'd willingly risked people's lives for the chance to build her following.

The monkey-man settled down on his haunches and wrapped his long simian arms round himself for comfort. He rocked back and forth, softly singing to himself, words that might have had meaning once but were now just a vague memory. Tariq felt overwhelmed and afraid. He couldn't help him. He couldn't help any of them.

Foriz grabbed Tariq's wrist and squeezed it until he winced. She was angry, angry like he'd never seen her before. 'Your Imix did this. Your great *hero*. Now what are you going to do, Tariq?'

'I'll . . . speak with her. Now we have two stones she'll have enough power to change them back. I know she will. Imix only . . .' he looked around at the pitiful monsters, '. . . only wants the best.'

Foriz scoffed. 'The trouble with people who pretend to have all the answers is they never admit it when they're wrong. This is Imix's dirty secret. She won't thank you for discovering it. It'll make you her enemy.'

'Then what do you suggest?' He wanted Foriz to be wrong, but why had Imix kept these poor creatures hidden? Because she was ashamed of her failure – it made sense. Imix wasn't the sort to appear weak or lacking. Everyone followed her because they believed she had all the answers. Him included.

Foriz pointed back towards the tunnel. 'Let's leave. We'll find the other two and get out of here. Back to New Ethrial and a ship away. Far away. And never come back. If Imix wants Dandaka, let her have it. It's not worth the risk.'

'I'm not running away! My parents are here. There are good people in Xibalba. Working together we could do some real good. I'm not giving up on that.'

'Look around you, Tariq!' Foriz grabbed him and dragged him to the nearest cage, one with a pig-man hybrid inside. 'This is what awaits you. This. No world of happy frolicking children where everyone's best friend is a wolf. Wolves are predators. That's their nature. You can't make friends with them! You pet a wolf and you're likely to get your throat ripped out. The wilderness is untamed, and it's savage, full of death and violence.

It's survival of the fittest. It's all howls and screams. We can't stay.'

His recurring vision was making awful sense now. People turned into animals everywhere. Maybe that was what Imix hoped to do now she had access to both spiritstones. Was she planning to transform everyone into beasts?

Tariq clutched his head. There was so much spinning around his mind he felt dizzy. 'Let's find Livia and Artos. Then we'll make a plan. We'll keep this secret for now. Agreed?'

Foriz wasn't happy but nodded. 'All right. But the moment it all blows up I'm leaving and I'll be leaving fast. Got it?'

CHAPTER 22
TARIQ

Lying on the flat roof of his house that night, gazing up at the stars, Tariq tried to make sense of it all. Foriz was curled up in the corner, asleep but fitfully. They needed to stick together. And they needed to find Artos and Livia. Where were they?

He'd spent the day asking around and no one knew. But no one was worried. He'd mentioned it to his parents, and they'd said if the others weren't back by the morning, they'd go looking for them.

Tariq didn't tell them about the cages and the miserable creatures trapped within them. He knew he could trust his parents, but if he'd told them, they would have wanted to bring it up with Imix and he wasn't so sure about her now. Hiding her failures was dishonest. More than dishonest, it was a betrayal. Weren't they all meant to be equal?

Imix loved presenting herself as the wise one, a priest queen of the past. Did she think those creatures made her appear less than perfect? Why did it matter? No one was perfect. He'd looked for her, wanting to confront her and learn the truth, but she'd ventured off to the river and no one knew when she'd be back.

If only he could find the others. He was starting to—

Tariq heard a soft squeak from nearby. There was a small brown mouse staring at him.

'Hello. I've some cheese downstairs if you fancy it.'

The mouse rubbed its face with its forepaws. 'I *squeak squeak* hate cheese.'

Tariq sat up. 'Did you squeak . . . I mean, *speak*?'

'You *squeak* understand me?' asked the mouse. 'It's me, Tariq. *Squeak* Livia!'

He turned as he heard a deep grunt from the shadows at the top of the stairs. Moonlight shone on the spiky bristles of a boar. It shook its head side to side. 'Imix turned us into *snort* animals.'

Tariq stared at the boar and its blue eyes. 'Artos? Is that you?'

The boar bobbed its great head. 'Sadly it is. *Oink.*'

The mouse scurried closer and Tariq held out his hand. It climbed on to his palm and looked straight at him. 'Imix turned us into animals and she's planning to do the same with everyone in New Ethrial. She's got the power to now, thanks to the World's Egg. It's amplifying the abilities she's gained from the Crocodile's Tear. You *squeak* have to admire the irony of it!'

Foriz yawned. 'Who are you yammering to? I'm trying— There's a boar up here.'

Artos snorted at her.

Foriz reached slowly for the dagger lying beside her. 'Easy, little piggy.'

'Leave the dagger alone,' warned Tariq. 'That's Artos. And this . . .' he held up his palm, displaying the mouse crouched on his palm, '. . . is Livia. Imix has transformed them into animals.'

Foriz rubbed her eyes. 'I must still be sleeping.'

He stared at his two friends, the tiny nervous mouse and the bristling, brutish boar. He wondered if he was still sleeping too – that would be the simplest explanation – but he was awake in Xibalba, and this was a place of the strangest magic and mysteries. But the mystery of the mouse and the boar needed solving. Right now.

Tariq stood up. 'I have to change them back.'

'How?' asked Foriz.

'With this?' Tariq took out the World's Egg. The spiritstones were connected. Could he tap into the power of the Crocodile's Tear with his own spiritstone?

He sat cross-legged with the World's Egg resting in his hands. Livia and Artos drew closer.

Artos sniffed the spiritstone. 'You think this *snort* will *snort* work?'

Tariq had tapped into the World's Egg from a distance that night of the attack on New Ethrial, so it was possible in principle. After all, the legends said the ancient seers had been able to access the powers of the spiritstones from *anywhere*. 'Only one way to find out,' said Tariq, and he closed his eyes.

He slowed down his breathing, taking deeper, longer breaths as if he was sinking. Sinking into himself, into the world. Breath was the wind. His heartbeat was the rumble of an earthquake, the heat of his body radiating the sun and the rushing of blood in his veins the river of life. He contained the elements within him. But he could feel the power of the Crocodile's Tear as well. He had teeth, nails, hair, the limbs with which to hunt or flee. He was both a mortal and a beast; what was the difference really?

Everything was connected. What he needed to do was manipulate those connections, the way he had done with the tidal wave.

He pictured Livia and Artos, as elf and as korr –
not just paying attention to the blueness of Artos's
eyes or the straight-backed posture of Livia, but
deeper. What made them who they were. Warrior.
Engineer. Loyal friends. Rebels. Heroes.

He concentrated on their essence, pushing
towards restoring them to their true selves.

But the more he concentrated, the more he saw
a timid mouse and a brooding boar.

Tariq's eyes sprang open. He gasped and shook
his head, exhausted by the effort. 'I can't. I haven't
developed a connection with it. That or Imix has a
stronger link and she's blocking me.'

Livia ran up his arm and nestled on his shoulder
right by his ear. 'Then we need to get the Crocodile's
Tear.'

'Imix isn't going to just hand it over,' said Artos.

Tariq turned towards Foriz. 'Then it's good
we've got a thief with us.'

They reached the top of the steps without
problem, the bright full moon illuminating their
path with its silvery light. Tariq carried Livia in his
pocket, but once they reached the plateau in front

of the entrance, he took her out and she sniffed the weathered stone.

'That was so embarrassing,' she said. 'Carried in a *squeak* pocket!'

Artos grunted as he shook his powerful shoulders. 'This stays between us. Once we're back in our *oink* normal *oink* . . . normal *oink oink* . . .'

They needed to be transformed back soon. The longer they remained as animals, the greater the risk they would forget they'd ever been mortals. Tariq joined Foriz, who was spinning her dagger between her fingers as she gazed into the doorway.

'So far, so good,' said Tariq.

'That's what worries me.' She pointed her weapon at the ominous opening. 'Why make it so easy? Imix must suspect we want the Crocodile's Tear.'

'She trusts everyone.'

Foriz smirked. 'That is a big mistake.'

Tariq patted his satchel, checking the World's Egg was in there. It was beginning to become a habit. He was worrying about it more and more. So much power in such a simple piece of stone.

Easily lost. Easily stolen. He was responsible for the spiritstone.

He looked back at the boar and mouse. How could Imix transform his friends against their will? He wanted to confront her, learn her reasons. But choices had to be made. He stood by his friends.

They went in.

He peered into the darkness and took a deep breath.

Fire. One of the elements that made the world. He felt the heat around him, rising from the jungle. There was energy flowing all around; he just needed to redirect it a little, focus it until . . .

Sparks danced in the fire pits. A few caught the dried moss and brittle twigs and became flames. It wasn't the spectacular eruption of fire Imix had generated but a steady spreading of light, one pit at a time, throughout the ancient cave.

The paintings seemed to move as the light grew. Animals roamed the walls, an illusion created by the unsteady light. This was what it must have been like when the ancient folk had first painted them. Too much light and the magic vanished. It needed shadows to work.

Livia squeaked and rushed into a crack in the wall.

'Livia? What's wrong?'

'*Oink*,' said Artos, lowering his head and squaring his heavy shoulders for a charge.

The cave was big and uneven, with alcoves and ledges all around. In the growing firelight a shape rose up from one of the upper ledges.

The silver gorilla.

Foriz swapped the dagger from hand to hand. 'Ah, now that's more like it.'

The huge ape climbed down from the ledge and landed with a splash in a puddle, then lumbercd to the middle of the cave and waited, leaning back and forth on its chunky knuckles, growling softly.

Artos took a few steps forward. The firelight shone on his wicked tusks.

Foriz circled to the side, the dagger blade glinting. 'Artos, you distract it. I'll get behind, then go in.'

'*Snort*.'

'I'll take that as a "yes",' said Foriz, her eyes never leaving the gorilla. 'Tariq, you couldn't summon a lightning bolt or something?'

'No, I'm not sure that's how it works.'

She shrugged. 'Just thought I'd ask.'

With the World's Egg he could affect the elements of nature. Not just fire, but air, water and . . . rock.

The ceiling was covered in stalactites. Some were the size of tree trunks, others no longer than his fingers. The gorilla was beneath one. He didn't want to kill the beast, but a bang to the head might knock it out long enough for them to grab the Crocodile's Tear and run.

'Foriz, you go and get the Tear. I'll deal with the gorilla.'

Foriz frowned at him. 'You really think you can handle that monster?'

'Just go.'

She tucked her dagger back into its sheath, then darted amongst the hundreds of stalagmites. She simply vanished within an eyeblink. Once a thief, always a thief.

The gorilla stood up and beat its chest as it roared out its challenge.

Artos lowered his head and charged.

Teeth gritted, Tariq turned his attention to the stalactite overhead. He sensed the hundreds of tiny grooves, minute cracks and breaks within the spear of rock. All he needed to do was find one and make it bigger until it broke. He reached out towards it, using the World's Egg to connect with the element of stone. Despite the distance, he made himself believe he and the stalactite were joined.

There was a crack, just about wide enough to slip his hand through. Tariq could feel the rough stone against his palm as he imagined pushing his hand in. He added power, forcing the crack to widen. It creaked as it created a dozen minor fractures that spread out through the stalactite.

Tiny shards of limestone fell over the gorilla, but it was too busy roaring at Artos to notice.

The boar slammed into the ape, who grabbed its head before those lethal tusks could tear it open.

'We don't want to kill it, Artos!' Tariq yelled.

Artos wriggled out of the gorilla's grip and headbutted it. The gorilla stumbled, then swung its fist into Artos's ribs. Artos squealed as he was sent tumbling.

The stalactite cracked free with the sound of thunder. The gorilla looked up but too late. It just had enough time to cover its head with its powerful arms before the rock smashed down on top of it.

The dust settled, revealing the gorilla, unconscious, lying amongst a dozen chunks of broken limestone.

Tariq helped Artos to his feet, and the boar oinked in thanks. The mouse scurried out of her hole and leapt up into Tariq's palm. He tucked her away in his pocket again.

'Foriz?' Tariq yelled, his shout echoing around the great temple cave.

'You'd better come here,' she shouted back.

He was so tired. Using magic exhausted him. Not just physically but mentally too. He struggled on, weaving through the winding passageway towards the chamber of the Crocodile's Tear, where he found Foriz waiting.

She tapped the flat of the dagger against her chin. 'Notice something?'

The alcove where the Tear was kept, it was empty.

CHAPTER 23
LIVIA

'Imix *squeak* has gone to New Ethrial,' said Livia.

It was getting harder and harder to concentrate. Or concentrate on anything but running, hiding and nibbling. She craved seeds, and she was desperate for somewhere to hide. Everything was too big, too terrifying. Even Tariq was monstrously huge! As a mouse, she was so fragile and afraid of being trod on, which was why she decided to stay in Tariq's pocket. She trembled constantly. Her heart skipped a beat with every noise. But then her heart rate was so high that it thrummed.

Think, Livia, think!

Nesting. Hiding. Running. Nibbling. Seeds. Nuts. A bread crust. Run and hide. Run and hide. That was the life of a mouse. That was all it thought about.

Tariq sat down and put her on his knee. 'New Ethrial? Why?'

'*Squeak squeak squeak*. Transform everyone. Turn them into snails, dogs, mice, anything and *squeak* everything.'

Foriz grimaced. 'She's had who knows how long a head start. How will we catch her?'

Tariq weaved his palm through the air. 'I could swim there. And . . . and you're not gonna like this, Livia, but you could hitch a lift. My dad could take you there in no time at all.'

'Your dad? How would he *squeeeeak*? *Squeeeak!*'

'From here to New Ethrial isn't far . . . as the eagle flies.'

He wanted her to be carried by an eagle? Livia

219

trembled from nose to tail. Its claws! What if it squeezed her too tightly? She would be crushed! What if it didn't squeeze her enough and she fell? She'd be smashed to a pulp! What if it got hungry mid-flight? Eagles ate mice! Most animals did!

And what use would she be if she got there? No, she was just a small mouse, frightened of everything. She needed to hide.

Tariq turned to Artos. 'It's a long way through the jungle.'

'*Oink*. Point me in the right direction and I'll be there. I am not *snort* letting Imix get away with this. I'm an *oink* Silver Guard!'

'What about you, Foriz?' asked Tariq. 'I know this isn't your fight, but we could do with your help.'

'It'll take me a while to get there on my two legs, but I've got a surprise or two.'

*

Tariq's mum, Miriam, stared at Livia as she nibbled a biscuit. 'Imix did *what*?'

They were all in Tariq's parents' hut. Artos paced around the room, snuffling in the corners, squealing and shaking his head. Livia sat on a wooden plate with her meal. She was so hungry! Mice burnt so much energy; their lives were entirely dominated by eating. She was struggling to think about anything else, to remember she was Livia, an elf apprenticed at the Guild of Artificers. Soon she'd forget she'd been anything but a mouse, and Artos would be a boar and nothing more.

Tariq looked worried. Poor Tariq. 'She changed Livia into a mouse and Artos into a boar. She's planning worse, Mum. We have to stop her!'

Nazir leaned against the wall, arms crossed. 'But how? Imix doesn't have that sort of power.'

Tariq raised his satchel. 'She's tapping into the World's Egg. She told us that the spiritstones amplify each other's powers. I shouldn't have brought it here.'

Mum snapped her fingers. 'Then can't you do the same? Tap into the Crocodile's Tear and change them back?'

Tariq shook his head. 'I've tried. I can't make a connection. I don't know if it's because I'm not familiar with the Tear or because Imix is blocking me.'

'Imix possessed all three stones once. She would have learnt how to maximise their powers,' said Nazir. 'I just . . . This isn't what we intended. She's gone too far.'

'There's worse,' said Tariq, looking towards Foriz. 'Imix has got other seers, ones who failed to fully transform, caged in a cave in the jungle.'

Both older seers stared at him, horrified. Nazir shook his head. 'She said they'd left. That there was nothing for them here in Xibalba. She said she'd use the Crocodile's Tear to change them, then send them on their way.'

Miriam grimaced. 'It sounded too good to be true, but who were we to doubt Imix and her powers?' She broke another biscuit and sprinkled it on to the plate for Livia. 'We have to hope Imix can transform your friends back.'

Livia scurried towards Tariq. 'Hope? You mean I'll be *squeak* stuck like this *squeak* forever! *Squeak!*'

Miriam frowned. 'I've heard stories about this. It used to be a punishment within the clans, back when the seers were more powerful. If they're not turned back soon, they'll forget they were ever anything but animals.'

'How long do we *snort* have?' asked Artos.

Mum bit her lip. 'With magic as powerful as Imix's? A couple of days? It's impossible to be sure.'

Tariq gazed down at her sympathetically. 'One thing at a time. We need to get to New Ethrial *fast*.'

Nazir and Miriam looked at each other. What were they thinking? They'd spent years here supporting Imix, following her lead. Would they really fight against her if it came down to it?

Miriam went to the door. 'We need to do this ourselves. Many others here would actually agree with Imix. Plenty would do whatever she asked, no questions.'

Tariq looked from one parent to the other. 'You're willing to take on Imix because of me?'

Miriam ruffled his hair. 'What a silly question.'

Nazir's hearty, chesty laughter filled the stone

room. He squatted down on his haunches and gazed at Livia. 'Fancy a trip?'

Livia shivered. *Squeeeak! Squeeeak!* The mouse wanted to flee, but the mouse wasn't in charge, not yet. Livia – the elf from Ethrial, who built wonderful machines, whose mind hadn't quite surrendered to animal instincts – knew this was the only way. She shuffled towards Nazir and brushed against his fingers.

Nazir smiled at her. 'I'll keep you safe.'

There was a growl from the panther as it paced at the doorway impatiently. Miriam was eager to be off.

Nazir spread out his arms and gave them a shake. Feathers began sprouting out of his skin as his arms transformed into wings. He gritted his teeth as his mouth metamorphosed into a beak. He shrieked as the last vestiges of his mortal self faded and a large golden eagle stood in his stead.

Those talons looked deadly! If the eagle squeezed too much she'd be sliced in half.

Tariq crouched down beside her. 'It'll be OK, Livia.'

She had to do this. She couldn't let the mouse win.

The eagle stretched out a leg and curled its talons gently round her body. Then, with a single beat of its huge wings, it flew straight out of the doorway, brushing the head of the jaguar. Another wingbeat and it soared over the cluster of houses. Yet another mighty wingbeat took it high over Xibalba.

The wind roared and the world swirled beneath her. Livia thought her heart might *explode* with the thrill of it. The lake was vast and she saw the silver tendrils of water spreading out in all directions through the moonlit jungle. The eagle did a long lazy swoop to the west, towards the sea, towards New Ethrial.

And Imix.

CHAPTER 24

ARTOS

Now that was a smell he recognised.

Vulcanite.

It was the smell of home. Of crowded city streets, of factories, of machines grinding, turning, chugging away and belching smoke to mix with the sea air of Ethrial. How he'd missed it!

All this fresh air? Who needed it?

Artos had run through half the night. Really run. He had the stamina for long distance but not the speed. The boar had both. He'd torn through the foliage, shaking broken twigs and clumps of leaves off his tusks, ripping apart the dangling vines, splashing through streams and bounding over fallen trunks. His sense of smell was so much sharper. This close to the ground he couldn't see where he was going but he could *smell* the path. Sniff his way to New Ethrial. He knew he was near. You couldn't mistake the scent of vulcanite, and there was only one vulcanite engine this side of the ocean.

The Harvester.

He heard the rumbling noise of its engine coming from beyond the edge of the forest ahead.

He continued on until, emerging from the trees, he found a field of stumps spread out before him. The earth had been torn up. Trees lay in the mud. Their branches had been shorn off and the trunks lay in rough irregular stacks waiting for transport.

Patches of foliage smouldered, all part of the clearing process. Smoke hung miserably over the carnage.

An orangutan wandered amongst the stumps. With no trees to swing through it looked clumsy and lost, searching for fruit from the fallen boughs.

Artos trotted through the churned-up mud, following the smell of the vulcanite and the drone of the engine. It was coming from the edge of the field amongst a wall of trees.

Moonlight shone on the axe blades. Smoke chugged out from the exhausts, as the engine continued to grumble and shake. One of the six legs had snapped off and was half buried in a ditch.

The Harvester, Livia's pride and joy, lay on its side like a broken beetle, three legs still twitching.

There was a suit of mud-smeared armour lying beside the broken leg. A silver sword jutted from the ground with a chicken perched on its hilt.

'Is that *snort* you, Febian?' said Artos. 'It's me, Artos.'

'Artos?' The chicken flapped its wings in panic. '*Cluck! Cluck!* What's *cluck* happened to me?'

'Let me guess, you *snort* bumped into Imix?'

228

The chicken stared at him. 'An old korrish woman came *cluck* out of the jungle while I was *cluck cluck* clearing the trees. She was angry.'

Artos glanced around at the stumps, the stacks of logs, the burning brush. 'I can see why. *Snort.*'

The chicken flapped down and began pecking at him. 'Do something, Artos! I'm a *cluck* chicken!'

'I'll be honest, I'm not that *snort* surprised.'

The chicken peered at him. 'What do you *cluck* mean, not that *cluck* surprised?'

'I suppose if you'd been asked what type of animal you'd be, you would have probably said . . . a lion? Or a unicorn?'

The chicken flapped over and over the ground. 'Do something! And, while you're at it, do you have any *cluck* seeds? I'm *cluck cluck* starving! *Cluck!*'

'Stay off the seeds, *snort*. Remember who and what you *snort* are. Really are.'

'*Cluck cluck!*'

Maybe some people adapted to their animal forms quicker than others? Artos needed to get moving.

'How *snort* far is the town?' he asked.

'*Cluck* a *cluck* kilometre?' said Febian the chicken.

The Harvester had ploughed a path through the jungle. A broad path of stumps and torn vegetation cut an almost straight line westwards.

'You wait here, Febian,' he said.

Febian didn't reply. He was busy pulling a worm from the soil.

Artos the boar trotted on.

CHAPTER 25
TARIQ

Tariq waded out of the river towards the bank and past the remains of the quayside. The wreck of a rowboat floated by.

He smelt the sea, still a few kilometres further downstream, and seagulls called overhead, like white ghosts gliding under the bright moonlight. He'd shape-changed into his eel form and swum as fast as he could. But Imix must have reached New Ethrial before him. Where was she?

A dog wearing a hat watched him from the riverbank. It looked at Tariq and whimpered.

Tariq was too late. Way too late. Imix had used her connection to the World's Egg to magnify her powers and transform . . . everyone.

He should have guessed. The vision was as clear as it could have been – people transformed into animals. Why had he thought only seers could shape-change?

Tariq climbed up the muddy bank and ruffled the dog's jowls. 'Do I know you?'

It barked.

Seagulls perched on the storage huts, flapping and crying out. Some were draped in torn clothing. A shirt or scarf and one that wore a necklace. Pigs scuffled along the barrels and bales. A group of monkeys were helping themselves to a crate of fresh mangoes. The town was a cacophony of animal cries, howls, barks and chatter. But there were no mortal voices. Not one.

An eagle swooped down out of the night and settled on the roof frame of a two-storey house. It shook its wings and a moment later there was Dad.

He climbed down and crossed the street, gazing around him. 'You were right, son. Imix has changed them all.'

'How's Livia?' asked Tariq.

Dad smiled as he opened up his hand. 'Ask her yourself.'

The mouse was swishing its tail and its whiskers were twitching excitedly. 'That was *squeak* amazing! Are we here?'

'We're at New Ethrial. Or what's left of it.'

Dad lowered Livia to the ground and she circled round them, sniffing and twitching.

'Any sign of Imix as you flew here?' Tariq asked.

Dad shook his head. 'But I can sense she's here, nearby.'

'We need to get the Crocodile's Tear off her any way we can. Then we'll use it to change everything back to how it was. Somehow.'

'It's not going to be easy,' said Dad. 'Imix is incredibly powerful and she's not going to just hand it over.'

'She's had it too long,' said Tariq. 'She's drawn on its power to extend her life, defying nature.

That was never the purpose of the spiritstones. They were meant to be used to maintain the balance between all things.'

Dad was grim. 'Including life and death.'

A chill ran down Tariq's spine. 'You think it'll come to that?'

Dad put his hand on Tariq's shoulder. 'A seer understands that spring gives way to winter. Things must end if there is to be new growth. Imix has forgotten that. We must remind her of what her purpose once was. If a seer does not live in accordance with nature and its cycles, then they are no true seer.'

It was unsettling, wandering around the town. The animals didn't know how to act. They hung on to their mortal nature, despite it no longer fitting their new forms. A few wore remnants of clothing or jewellery. There was a bear sitting on a chair, trying to eat some rice off a plate, growling as it couldn't quite hold a spoon in its giant paws. A horse with a skirt dangling from one hind leg neighed at them from the vegetable stall.

Livia darted back and forth, sniffing one alley and then the next. She squeaked as she came face to face with a ginger cat, but the cat meowed with fright and disappeared off down the alleyway.

They made their way to Lord Marius's mansion.

Someone was sitting at the dining table in the courtyard, sobbing. He wore a hat with a purple peacock feather.

'Lord Marius? Is that you?' said Tariq. He hadn't thought there was a single human person in all the town. 'What happened? Are you all right?'

The man stared at Tariq, so bewildered it took him a few moments to recognise the boy before him. 'Tariq? You're back. Oh, my boy, help me! I beg you! You can have all my gold, but please, I'm begging you, save me!'

Marius stumbled towards him but collapsed on the flagstone floor and sobbed. 'Save me . . .'

The reason he'd stumbled? His lower half was that of a goat. Imix had only half transformed him.

Tariq helped Lord Marius up on to a stone bench. 'Imix, where is she?'

'Right here,' came a voice from the balcony overlooking the courtyard. 'I've been waiting for you, Tariq.'

CHAPTER 26
TARIQ

'I wish you could understand what I want to do,' said Imix. 'How I can save the world.'

Tariq glanced back towards the town. 'If it's more of that, then I don't think I'll ever understand. Change them back, Imix.'

'Why? So they can carry on exactly as before? No, I don't think so. Now, to save a lot of hardship and pain for you just put the World's Egg on that table and leave. I'll give you that chance at least.'

'And what will you do with the Egg?'

'Bring balance back to the world. There are too many cities destroying the natural environment. Maybe an earthquake or two will slow things down. People need to learn to live close to the earth once more. Too much civilisation is bad. And despite what you've been told by your friend, you *can* stop progress.'

This was who Imix truly was. How could Tariq have been so wrong about her? How could she betray him like this? Betray all of them? Or did the other seers agree with her plans?

'I don't want to fight you, Imix,' said Tariq.

She smirked. 'You really don't, boy.'

He'd never wanted this. He'd hoped Imix would help him use the Crocodile's Tear to save them from the dangers ahead, never imagining she would use it to make things worse. Would it have been better if he'd never come searching for the spiritstone?

He'd only had the World's Egg a few months. Tariq knew it would take him a lifetime to discover all its secrets. But he had learnt something and he hoped it was enough.

There was only one way to find out.

The World's Egg had been a gift the ancient gods had given the elemental spirits, the spirits who controlled air, fire, water and earth. He'd tapped the connection to the water element to control the tidal wave that had come close to destroying Ethrial, but he needed to use another element to take on Imix.

Tariq took a deep breath, grounding himself. He felt the land beneath his feet, imagined himself spreading out . . . roots through the soil, expanding his connection to the earth. Down and down he went, into the rocks far below. He gave them a little push.

The ground shook, the pillars swayed and the walls quivered. It lasted a few moments before settling back, but by then there were some new cracks in the plaster and a few of the tiles on the floor had cracked.

Imix clapped. 'Very impressive, Tariq. It would be easier if we were working together. Give me the Egg.'

Tariq had to be careful, restrained. He had the

238

Egg. Imix had the Tear. Two stones close together, each amplifying the power of the other. There was no way he was going to let Imix have them both. 'I'd sooner throw it into the sea.'

'I'd find it, Tariq. There's a connection between the stones, between all three. I'm surprised you can't feel it. Once I have two, I'll seek out the third, the Heart's Desire. I have *such* plans for the world. To bring about a better age, one of perfect harmony.'

'With you as priest queen? Is that it?'

'Someone has to lead, and who better than me? We seers see the world as it is, and know how it should be. You've been brought up in a world that hates you, so you fear and despise that part of yourself. It's a tragedy. You should never be ashamed of who or what you are. If the world won't accept you, it can be made to.'

'By making them afraid of us? That's not a better world, that's tyranny.'

Imix jumped over the balcony railings. They were six or seven metres above the ground but as she fell, she spread out her arms and they transformed into golden-feathered wings. They fanned out almost five metres tip to tip, slowing her fall, and just before her toes touched the ground, she pulled her arms back in, the feathers disappearing in the blink of any eye. It had happened so fast Tariq couldn't quite believe what he'd seen.

Imix could not only change into other animals – she could take on their particular attributes as well. He'd thought her turning into a monstrous crocodile had been amazing enough. He should have guessed. Imix had studied the Crocodile's Tear for the last few centuries. She would have uncovered its deep secrets.

Imix snapped her fingers. 'How about a deal? Give me the Egg and I'll change your friends back to how they were. That seems fair.'

Livia scurried out of his pocket and up on to Tariq's shoulder. 'She's *squeak* lying!'

'Show me you can do it first,' said Tariq. 'Change Livia back right now.'

Marius wailed. 'No, me! Me first! I'm important! Imix, I'll give you everything you want! I'll leave

New Ethrial forever! Just change me back, I beg you!'

An ear-piercing shriek took Tariq's attention to the sky. Dad had transformed back into an eagle and was circling above the open courtyard, ready to take on Imix from the air. Then there was a deep threatening growl as a black panther prowled across the roof tiles, its golden eyes shining in the moonlight while its glossy fur rippled with raw power. *Mum*. It peeled back its lips to reveal deadly fangs.

Imix gazed at the two beasts. 'There's nothing more heart-warming than to see a family working together.'

The panther sprang off the roof on to the ground and landed in a crouch between Tariq and Imix. 'Imix, don't do this. Let's find another way,' it growled.

Imix shook her head. 'Miriam, I thought you of all people would understand. You were exiled from your clan. You know others are jealous of our powers; they always will be. Seers have served for long enough without thanks. Now it is time for us to rule! Once I have the Heart's Desire, there will be . . . Well, that's for another time.'

'You know what the Heart's Desire is capable of?' Tariq asked.

Imix smirked. 'The three stones were once in my possession, but I was too timid to use them when I should have. But that was when I was younger, lacking the knowledge – courage – I needed. Now I know what to do, how to access the greatest powers of the stones, how to use them as they were meant to be used.'

Tariq had to stop her here, tonight.

Mum stalked up beside him, growling. Dad spread out his wings and Artos beat the flagstones with his hoof, swaying his head side to side, those tusks of his more deadly than any sword of the Silver Guard. He circled round Marius's dining table to get within charging distance of Imix.

The seer tied the Crocodile's Tear round her arm with a thick strip of leather, keeping it against her skin so she could access its powers more easily. Then she took a deep breath. 'It is a shame it has come to this.'

'*Squeak!*'

Tariq glanced down. 'Livia? You'd better find somewhere to hide.'

'*Squeak. Squeak.* I want to *squeak* fight too,' said the tiny brown mouse.

'Hmm. You sure about this?'

Livia's eyes shone. 'You just keep her busy.'

Tariq smiled. 'You have a cunning plan?'

'Of course I *squeak* do!' She scurried away.

Mum's claws scraped across the courtyard's flagstone floor as she circled Imix. 'We trusted you. Why betray everything you stood for?'

Imix just shrugged. 'Harsh times call for harsh methods, Miriam. You're a predator – can't you see when an animal is sick it's best to put it out of its misery? The same goes for society.' Imix turned her attention to Tariq. 'But children are naive. Too full of blind hope.'

'Leave the heavy fighting to us,' Artos grunted. The hairs on his shoulders bristled angrily. 'Imix! Enough talk! Let's *snort* do this!'

Imix spread out her arms. 'Come and get me.'

243

CHAPTER 27

ARTOS

Even as Artos charged, Imix transformed. How could she do it so quickly? In an eyeblink she was a cobra but giant-sized. Seven or eight metres long, with fangs the length of sabres glistening with yellow venom. One bite . . .

Imix launched herself at the boar, the snake's coils propelling her across the courtyard in an instant.

The eagle shrieked as it swooped, aiming to

gouge the snake's eyes with its talons, but the cobra ducked and Artos slammed into it.

It was like crashing into an oak tree! The cobra was solid muscle. He jammed his tusks into the scales, looking for a gap to get at the flesh underneath. The scales were tougher than the best armour, but Artos wasn't going to quit. He twisted, hooking the tips of his tusks between the scales, then shoved forward with all his strength, driving those tips in deeper.

The scales gave way to thick fur. A pair of huge hairy arms locked round Artos's sides and suddenly he was face to face with a bear. Was there anything Imix couldn't change into?

The bear roared as the panther bit deep into its leg. It dropped Artos and he backed away, gasping. Definitely a few broken ribs. It was hard to breathe properly and his head swam. The ground, the whole building, seemed to be tilting from side to side. He shook his head to clear the dizziness, but the ground was definitely moving . . .

Tariq was holding the World's Egg in both hands. The spiritstone glowed with a rainbow of colours, washing the courtyard in ever-changing light. The flagstones beneath the bear cracked open.

The bear became a hawk and with a single flap of its wings it darted up and out of the jagged chasm.

The eagle chased, shrieking its challenge.

The two raptors disappeared from the courtyard, heading away from the mansion.

'Come on!' yelled Tariq as he held out his hand for Livia. The mouse jumped on and the two of them ran out of the crumbling mansion.

The panther nudged him. 'Are you hurt, Artos?'

'*Snort!*'

The panther chuckled. 'You're as tough as they come. The battle's not over. Want to help me finish it?'

'*Snort snort.*'

The panther winked then ran off after the others.

Artos had thought it would be easier standing now he had four legs, but, no, not at all. He was bleeding along his torso. The bear had scraped its claws along his ribs and his black bristles were matted with blood.

So what? He was one of the Silver Guard. The Guard fought and bled for Ethrial. That was their job. They did it so others wouldn't have to. It didn't matter if Ethrial was a thousand kilometres away across the sea.

He didn't want to admit it to the others but he knew things weren't perfect back home. Ethrial was the greatest and richest city in the world. Then why, with all that wealth, were there so many homeless? People begging, children going hungry or else working in factories and even down mines when they should have been at school? Surely there was gold aplenty to fix all that?

He'd thought New Ethrial might start without those failures but he saw it was plotting the same path. All driven by greed. So he didn't care about its success, about creating a new colony for Ethrial to profit from.

And Artos did understand Imix's point of view. Was Imix's plan any more destructive than the mines, the factories and the pollution that were the cost of civilisation? Were the people in Ethrial any happier than they had been when it had just been a cluster of fishing villages?

There would be time to ponder that later. Even if he understood her thinking, he couldn't support Imix's plans and methods.

Swaying from side to side, his hoofs slipping on the smooth marble, Artos stumbled out of Marius's mansion.

'What about me?' shouted Lord Marius. 'What about me? I'm important! You have to do what I say!'

Artos looked over his shoulder. '*Snort.*'

Really, what else was there to say?

The eagle and hawk fought in the night sky. The eagle was bigger, the hawk faster. They shrieked as they swiped at each other with their talons and deadly hooked beaks, both ripping off feathers and trying to bring their foe crashing down to earth.

'Tariq!' Artos shouted. 'Help your dad!'

Tariq nodded and climbed up on to one of the single-storey houses. The seagulls perched on top squawked and flew off. Artos wondered if the house was theirs.

Tariq raised the World's Egg high.

The sails on the few remaining boats along the quay began to swell. The calm sea rippled and soon crests of waves rolled across the beach.

He was good, there was no denying it. Tariq had only had the World's Egg for a few months and already he could summon the elements at will.

A sudden gust of wind knocked the two birds apart, sending the lighter hawk spinning uncontrollably through the air. The eagle rallied first, its heavier mass and larger wings overcoming the air currents, closing in for the kill.

But just as its claws reached out for its prey, Imix switched. Hawk to viper. The snake sank its fangs into the eagle's leg.

The eagle cried out and tumbled to the earth.

The viper landed in a tree.

Artos and the panther ran to the fallen eagle. It lay there, flapping its wings as they transformed into arms, and the feathers retreated into the skin as it returned back to human, back into Tariq's dad.

'*Snort?*' asked Artos.

Nazir was looking pale. He winced as he locked his hands above the fang punctures in his calf. 'Just . . . just stop Imix.'

The panther snarled in response, then turned to the tree into which the viper had fallen and with a single leap launched itself up into the branches.

But, as ever, Imix was one step ahead. The leaves shook violently as the panther tumbled out and crashed against a wall, swiftly followed by a squat gorilla. Before the panther could recover, the gorilla lifted it overhead and hurled it into the bushes.

Artos charged in, slamming into the gorilla's back, catapulting it towards the river. The moment it got up, Artos charged into it again, and again. Each impact shook him to his bones, but if it was bad for him it was worse for the gorilla. He couldn't give Imix time to change. She was getting slower, taking longer to recover. She was growing tired.

Another thunderous charge sent the gorilla tumbling down the riverbank and into the water with a huge splash.

Artos stood on shaky legs, panting. His chest heaved and the hairs across his shoulders bristled. Now he knew why he'd been changed into a boar. He loved fighting.

Imix, back in mortal form, rose out of the water, spluttering. Artos stood at the top of the riverbank, snorting, daring her to come up.

But Imix started wading in deeper. She sank into the river and disappeared.

Artos went down the slope cautiously. He walked along the river's edge. Where was she? He turned as Tariq slid down the muddy slope.

'You want to go in and get her?' asked the river boy.

'*Snort* not *snort* really,' said Artos. 'Though maybe she's turned into a *oink* little fish?'

Tariq chuckled. 'You really think so?'

Artos snorted.

'Crocodile, then,' said Tariq, peering hard at the still surface of the water.

'What else?' said Artos. 'Let's *snort* keep away from the edge. That'll force her to come to us. On the ground we'll *snort snort* have the advantage.'

'Unless she changes again.'

Artos shook his tusked head. 'She's slower. Those last few cost her. We can't let her *snort* recover. You need to get the *snort* Crocodile's Tear off *snort* her.'

Tariq nodded. 'Let's get out of—'

'Look out!' Artos smashed into Tariq, knocking him three metres away as the crocodile sprang out of the water. It twisted and tried to grab at Tariq as he tumbled along the muddy riverbank. If Artos hadn't batted him away, Tariq would have been in the crocodile's gullet. It tried a second time, but Artos barged between them to protect the boy.

The crocodile hesitated. It had learnt to be wary of Artos.

That's what the Silver Guard did. They guarded. Artos wasn't going to let the crocodile get his friend.

And the huge reptile knew it. It backed away, slithering slowly into the water.

CHAPTER 28
TARIQ

'She's getting away!' squeaked Livia.

Imix was still in her giant crocodile form. Of all the beasts she could change into, the crocodile was her most powerful. She was daring them to come after her.

Tariq ran to the riverside and hurled his satchel towards Artos. 'Look after this!'

He dived in. The moment he was submerged he began changing.

It was still shocking, despite it being his third time transforming. And it was just as painful as before. His muscles spasmed and each bone mutated into a vastly different skeleton. Tariq's vision, usually blurry underwater, slowly began to focus. He risked a breath and was rewarded with air filtering through the gills that lined his throat on either side of his jaw. He reached out to make another stroke but his instinct was to undulate now. He had no limbs but a supple serpentine body with powerful muscles perfectly designed for sliding through water.

Imix was heading upstream, back to Xibalba. He could feel the power of the Crocodile's Tear. She was drawing on it, but so much power was radiating out of it that Tariq felt it too, making him stronger. But would he be strong enough to take on Imix?

She would show no mercy. He needed to draw more power from the Tear if he was to have any chance of beating her.

There. Ahead. A huge dark shape was gliding through the water just below the surface. The moonlight glinted on its knobbly scales. She didn't know he was coming. Who would be fool enough to chase Imix?

Tariq smirked. This was the sort of thing Artos would do. Maybe he was picking up some of his friend's iron-headed tenacity! But he also needed some of Livia's cleverness. He wouldn't win a straight fight, and there was no way to avoid fighting.

Even as he drew closer, the energy of the Tear flooded through Tariq, amplifying his eel form. He was swelling in size and . . . He tingled. Every few moments he'd twitch and a strange energy surged through his core, expanding outwards to send a shiver across his skin.

What had Livia called it? Electricity? The eels in the river here were able to produce electric jolts that stunned their victims.

But those attacks were on small fish, not an armour-plated crocodile.

The crocodile swam through a glade of long water weeds. The other inhabitants fled: fishes darted into hiding places within the riverbank, frogs burrowed into the mud and a large pike, a hunter in its own right, slipped down into a hole at the bottom.

As the crocodile drifted round a bend in the river it slowed, and for a brief moment the moonlight cutting through the water fell on the Crocodile's Tear tied securely to the beast's left forelimb. As Tariq grew closer, still unseen, he felt another more powerful shock run through him from his snout to the tip of his tail. His nerves buzzed and his strength multiplied the closer he got to Imix and the stone dangling from her leg. If this was how he felt, how much stronger was she?

But faced with such a towering threat, he asked himself, what would Artos do?

What else? Tariq gave one savage flick and suddenly was on Imix. He snapped his jaws on her leg, his needle-sharp teeth piercing the thick hide, drawing blood.

Imix spun round, churning the water and silt, turning the clear water murky. The crocodile's jaws widened and Tariq let go just as they snapped shut. Any slower and he'd have been bitten in half.

There was a moment of recognition in the crocodile's eyes – it was surprised he had dared attack it – before it launched into a full, frenzied attack, determined to rip Tariq to bloody chunks. He twisted and wriggled frantically, consumed by the fear of being bitten in half by those immense jaws.

The charge within him was building, making him tingle. But he couldn't get close enough to use it. The crocodile's frenzied attacks seemed to come from all directions. It tried to catch him with its jaws, then would lash with its tail, churning more and more silt. Visibility was down to nothing.

Then Tariq flicked his tail across the crocodile's snout as it came charging out of the cloudy water. It was a light touch, but he shuddered as he released the built-up electricity. The water was suddenly lit up by a blue flash and the crocodile spasmed, its body thrashing uncontrollably.

He'd stunned it!

But Tariq was exhausted. The shock had drained him. He could barely move and was sinking. He needed to hide while he regained his strength, so slithered down amongst a dense patch of weeds.

Eventually the crocodile stopped twitching as the shock subsided. It snapped its jaws angrily, twisting through the water, searching for him.

The Crocodile's Tear dangled from its leg only a short distance away. He could dart for it, bite it off. It was so close . . .

She wants me to go for it. She can't find me, so she's . . . fishing.

He shivered as the electric charge began to build up again. That last strike had stunned the crocodile. What if he waited longer before attacking? Could he stun it for longer, even knock it out? The crocodile was massive but he didn't know what his limits were.

The Crocodile's Tear glowed a bright emerald green.

It was so close . . .

He couldn't wait. He wasn't ready but he didn't have a choice.

Tariq launched out of his hiding place amongst the weeds.

The crocodile twisted instantly. One moment it was heading away and then, with a single thunderous thrash of its tail, it had turned round and had its jaws wide open, a metre away.

Tariq twisted as they snapped shut, and cried in pain as the crocodile's teeth bit into his tail, holding him fast. Then it surged out of the water, turned over and swung Tariq through the air to smash him down on the surface.

Everything turned black.

CHAPTER 29
TARIQ

Tariq had blacked out; it was only for a moment but even a moment was too long. The crocodile wasn't letting go. It flipped into another bone-crunching roll and smashed Tariq down on the water's surface again. He couldn't take much more. As the crocodile twisted a third time, Tariq fired out all his electricity. He didn't hold back. It was everything or nothing.

He pulsed with electricity over and over again.

The crocodile jerked but would not let go. Its jaws were clamped shut on his tail. They were locked together, the crocodile trying to stun Tariq into unconsciousness, Tariq trying to do the same. The harder one tried, the more the other fought back. Tariq was being thrown like a whip, every muscle stretched to breaking point. Much more and he'd be ripped apart.

He fired the last of his electricity and the crocodile spasmed uncontrollably and its jaws sprang open.

Tariq began to shape-change, his energy exhausted by that last electric shock. The riverbank was ten metres away. He didn't know how long the crocodile would remain stunned; the instant it recovered he'd be finished.

He dragged himself up into the air, gasping. He was trembling, his legs bleeding from the crocodile's grip on his tail. The sensible thing to do would be to retreat, get healed, leave this fight for another day. But in another day it would be too late. Everyone Imix had changed would be stuck as animals forever.

He couldn't abandon the fight. Tariq had to get the Crocodile's Tear.

He took a deep breath and went back under. He felt his way along the reptile's twitching body until he felt its front leg. Then he slid his palm along the scales until he touched the leather strap and the stone. He tugged. The spiritstone was tightly knotted in.

The crocodile shifted its head from side to side. It was beginning to regain control of its body.

He dug his nails into the knot, trying to force the leather binding apart, but there was hardly any give.

Come on, just a little bit looser . . .

Tariq grabbed hold of the stone with both hands and pushed against the crocodile with his feet.

Come on!

If only he had half Artos's strength, then this would be easy! Tariq twisted the knot from side to side, trying anything to undo it.

Then the crocodile shook violently along its full length. It beat the water with its tail and pulled away from Tariq suddenly. The shock had worn off and it still had the Tear tied to its leg.

Tariq had failed and was too exhausted to change back. He was mortal and felt incredibly vulnerable as the crocodile surged towards him, its yellow eyes glimmering in the murk. He turned and swam for the riverbank.

The crocodile snapped at him. He felt its teeth scrape his bare heels. It thrashed the water to gain on him, even as Tariq crawled up the muddy slope.

The crocodile charged through the reeds along the riverbank, and he dived forward as the crocodile snapped again. Sliding over the mud and leaves, Tariq frantically tried to put more distance between them, tripping over hidden roots, smacking into low branches and struggling through the dense foliage – and on and on came the crocodile, barging through all obstacles.

He wasn't going to make it! Any moment now and the crocodile would have him. It was over . . .

'Tariq! This way!'

He spun, bewildered at where the voice was coming from. 'Foriz?'

She stepped out from behind a tree, beckoning him frantically. 'This way!'

Tariq sprinted towards her, the crocodile at his heels. As he burst through some bushes, Foriz grabbed him and pulled him aside. Tariq was gasping, limbs aching. 'The crocodile . . .'

Foriz smiled wickedly. 'I brought some friends who can take care of Imix.'

The darkness around them erupted into a cacophony of screams, roars, howls and other hideous, unnatural cries. Swinging down from the trees, bounding and slithering out of the shadows, came the hybrids, those seers who'd been trapped between one shape and another. Foriz had freed them.

With their claws and fangs bared, they surrounded the giant crocodile.

They had come for revenge.

CHAPTER 30
TARIQ

'Sorry I'm late,' said Foriz. 'Some of them weren't too keen to leave their cages.'

'How did you persuade them?' Tariq asked.

Foriz smirked. 'Oh, I told them they'd have their revenge on Imix.'

The crocodile circled warily, snapping its jaws at any of the hybrids who got too close. But Imix was surrounded and the pitiful half-changed creatures edged nearer, growling, snarling and howling at her, their eyes blazing with feral rage.

The crocodile lashed out at a hybrid gorilla person with her immense tail, but the hairy beast swung itself up on to a branch out of harm's way.

A jackal creature darted forward and sank its teeth into the crocodile's front leg, tearing at its scales, and suddenly others followed suit, screaming in rage at what Imix had done to them. She'd promised these seers the great gift of transformation but left them trapped.

The crocodile fought back. It snapped its jaws round the torso of a serpent man and flung him into a pack of monkey creatures.

Tariq watched, horrified, as the hybrids tore at the crocodile in a frenzy of violence. He'd seen wolves take down a stray deer, and he'd gone out with the hunters of his clan when they'd come across a herd of oxen roaming through the forest. He'd caught plenty of fish and small animals himself for Nani's pot. That was survival, plain and simple. This was pure savagery.

'We need to call them off,' he said to Foriz.

'Why? Let them have their revenge, Tariq. Then you can pluck the Crocodile's Tear from her corpse.'

'I don't want Imix dead. We need her to change everything back to how it was,' said Tariq.

'And how are you going to do that?'

'With Imix's help.'

Tariq knew how to use the World's Egg, but not the Crocodile's Tear. If there was any chance of transforming everyone back to their original forms, he needed Imix to show him how. Somehow he had to persuade her to help.

'Call them off!'

Foriz frowned, then nodded abruptly. She put two fingers between her lips and released an ear-piercing whistle.

But the fight raged on. The crocodile slapped two more beast creatures into a tree and flattened another as it rolled over it. The gorilla beast beat the crocodile with a large branch and a serpent hybrid sank its fangs into the crocodile's tail, ripping through its thick hide.

'Call them off!' Tariq cried again.

'They're not listening!' Foriz whistled again – louder, longer – but the beasts, all of them, were lost to their rage. It was going to turn into slaughter.

And then . . . there was a squeal, the battle cry of a warrior.

Charging through the bushes came a boar with a mouse riding on its back.

'Now that's not something you see every day,' said Foriz.

The mouse tumbled off the boar's back a moment before Artos headbutted the crocodile so hard the giant reptile slid back a metre.

'What are they doing?' shouted Foriz. He wasn't sure but he trusted Artos and Livia. The tiny brown mouse burst out from a pile of leaves and leapt on to the tip of the crocodile's tail while it was shaking its head from the impact of Artos's attack.

Tariq's blood chilled. One false move and Livia would be crushed, but she was the only chance they had.

The other hybrids dashed back and forth, threatening the crocodile then darting out of reach as it turned on them. It couldn't decide who to chase.

The mouse raced along Imix's back and down the crocodile's forelimb, heading towards the glowing Crocodile's Tear. She was too small, too light for the reptile to even notice her.

'You can do it,' Tariq whispered. Livia was so close!

He didn't know how she hung on. The crocodile was twisting and turning this way and that, yet the mouse bit into the leather knot and clung on desperately, even as the crocodile charged towards a bear with a man's head. The bear man grabbed the crocodile's snout and roared as it tried to squeeze its jaws closed.

The mouse bit through the first strip of leather. Now the spiritstone only dangled by a single strip.

The bear man shoved the crocodile on to its back and it flailed its legs frantically, trying to right itself.

The mouse flew off.

'Livia!' Tariq yelled.

Foriz shoved him aside. 'I'll get her! You go get the stone!'

The spiritstone!

The Crocodile's Tear lay in the dirt, glowing but ignored, as the crocodile fought on.

Tariq ran, then slid, weaving between the terrifying reptile and the raging hybrid. One whack from Imix's tail or one swipe from the bear's paws and he'd be out till next week. He rolled under the scrum, reached out for the Crocodile's Tear . . .

And grabbed hold of it.

CHAPTER 31
TARIQ

The Crocodile's Tear was warm, as if alive. Tariq let its heat spread through him, allowing himself to absorb the energy radiating from the spiritstone – and enter the world of beasts.

It was far, far beyond how he'd felt transforming into an eel, feeling the kinship with a single alternate form. Tariq was awakening to the knowledge that he was kin to all beasts. Those that swam, ran, crawled and flew.

His heart quickened. To be a deer, racing through the forest, bounding gracefully over the fallen logs, ears pricked up for any hint of danger.

His muscles swelled. To be a bear, to have that immense power. He lumbered steadily down to the river, licking his lips at the promise of salmon.

The wind roared in his ears as he spread his wide wings to be a soaring eagle, master of the sky.

He understood why Imix had taken her path.

But the more you shape-changed, the harder it was to come back. Back to your true self.

He sensed the magic coursing through Imix's crocodilian body, burying her mortal self under the knobbly skin of a giant reptile. Over the years she had become disconnected from her original self, giving in to the beast, the great all-devouring crocodile, more and more. She was in the same danger as all the others who'd been transformed – that she'd forget what she once had been and all that went with it.

There was an animal, a beast, in each of them. In everyone. But to give it free rein was dangerous. You would lose everything else. All the memories, all the feelings, all the loves and losses that made you who you were. A crocodile didn't feel, it didn't remember, it just hunted and hunted and hunted, detached from everything except its hunger, the emptiness deep inside that could never be filled. That was what made a monster.

Tariq needed to undo the lock that held the real Imix prisoner. He needed to transform the crocodile.

It was a skin that Imix wore. It wasn't her true form. He wanted Imix the seer, not this monster.

He pictured her, the old korrish woman with a thatch of wild white hair. He imagined how she walked, how she stood; her mannerisms, the expressions she wore, how she'd half close her eyes when she was narrating some ancient legend.

Green light erupted from the Tear, transforming the darkness into a blaze of emerald brilliance. The beast creatures screamed in fear and fled to the shadows of the jungle.

But the crocodile stayed and fought back.

Imix resisted the change. It wasn't a battle in the physical realm but in the spirit, each seer tapping into the powers of the spiritstone to beat their enemy.

Tariq was bombarded by images of the crocodile attacking him. He flinched at each snap of its jaws and shook as he was thrashed by its scaly tail. It wasn't actually happening but it was still *real*.

But he endured the crocodile's onslaught. Battered, bruised and broken, he would not give up. He delved deep into the Crocodile's Tear's powers, searching for a way to beat Imix, and then . . . there it was.

Imix hadn't been much older than he was now when she had first used the Crocodile's Tear to transform. The Crocodile's Tear had been a gift to be shared, to bring harmony to the world of beasts, mortals and elemental spirits. But Imix had used it to fulfil her own ambitions. She had tortured when she should have healed. Ruled when she should have supported. Greedily clung on when she should have let go. Her connection to the spiritstone was so strong he could sense it, like thick vine covering an ancient tree, binding it, choking it. But it was all rotten.

Tariq reached out to the brittle vine and tore it apart.

He opened his eyes and sighed. The light radiating from the Crocodile's Tear faded, revealing a frail old woman curled up in the dirt.

'What . . . what have you done to me?' said Imix, staring at her hands – her normal stub-fingered hands. She was covered in mud and leaves. She leaned against a tree trunk, eyes closed, fists clenched, concentrating. She took deep harsh breaths, then groaned.

She stared at the Crocodile's Tear in Tariq's hand. 'You've broken the connection I had with the stone. Give it back!'

Tariq wearily shook his head. 'Don't you think you've had it long enough?'

Imix's shoulders slumped with misery. 'You don't understand, Tariq. I need the Crocodile's Tear. I need its connection to . . . all things. To all the life in the jungle. I've been sharing it for so long. It keeps me alive.'

Tariq sat down. He'd never been so battered nor exhausted. The two spiritstones were a heavy burden. How could anyone bear their weight for this long? He looked up at Imix and realised how how tired she really was.

'You deserve to rest, Imix. Stop now and be remembered for all the good you did. You carry on and what'll be your legacy? You'll be remembered not as a wise woman but as a tyrant and monster. You'll have failed in the one thing that mattered most.'

'What's that?' asked Imix bitterly.

'To inspire us. The world. You could show us the way but you cannot lead us there, not any more. There is spring and then there is winter. There is a time for growing and for . . . returning.'

Imix slumped and buried her face in her hands. 'I'm so tired. It's gone on for so long but I don't know how to stop.'

Tariq stood up and held out his hand. 'Let me help.'

CHAPTER 32
TARIQ

'You really trusting her *oink* with *oink* this?' asked Artos. 'Who's to say she won't transform all of us, you included, into worms?'

'Imix is the only one with the knowledge to carry this out. Or are you happy to wait a few years while I learn how to use the Crocodile's Tear myself?' said Tariq.

Artos grunted. 'The moment she looks at me funny *snort* I'm going to headbutt her.'

'You do that. What about you, Livia?'

'*Squeak.*'

Tariq nodded. At least Livia trusted his decision.

They were in the small square of New Ethrial. The humans in animal form wandered around aimlessly. The hybrids were gathered by the riverside with Foriz.

The sun was rising, bleeding its light over the sea, and in the beautiful dawn Tariq saw that there was no going back, not for New Ethrial. He'd unleashed the power of the World's Egg and as well as cracks left by the tremors, the buildings along the seafront had been washed away. He'd need to be more careful.

'I'm not sure I can do this,' said Imix.

Even in this short time she'd aged. She now used a branch as a walking stick and paused every few paces to gather her breath. Her hair had fallen out in clumps, revealing a yellowed liver-spotted scalp. Her eyes were no longer bright but rheumy. She'd lost most of her teeth and her gums were pale and wrinkled, her cheeks puckered.

'I'll be here to help,' said Tariq.

Imix gazed out towards the sea. 'I had such plans, Tariq. Maybe too many. Funny, now I've stopped I feel as if a weight has come off my shoulders.' She glanced down at the two spiritstones on the ground between them. 'Careful, Tariq, they're heavier than they look. The weight of them might crush you.'

'I have friends to share the burden,' he replied.

Tariq helped Imix sit down on a discarded stool. Her knees clicked loudly as she bent down. Then she held the Crocodile's Tear in her palms and closed her eyes.

He sat down opposite and settled the World's Egg in his lap.

The spiritstones glowed softly. A few animals nearby whimpered, shuffling backwards as the light pulsed from both spiritstones – red, green, blue and yellow, weaving into each other until they became a single pure white light growing brighter, stronger with every beat of Tariq's heart. The two stones were working together, enhancing each other's powers.

Eyes closed, breathing slowly, deeply, Tariq

slipped into the world of the spirits. This world was a ghostly mirror of the real world, but alive in ways his normal senses could never detect. Much more alive. Alive and intertwined. He felt the energies of the World's Egg radiating out in all directions, guided through him. But it was not his responsibility to control those energies. The World's Egg was here to restore balance, not to serve his whims. The trees at the edge of town swayed. A sudden breeze brought with it the rich scent of blossom.

The wet soil underfoot sprouted saplings. The wide expanse of forest that had been chopped down for new buildings began regrowing. The jungle was reclaiming New Ethrial. Not over decades or even years but in moments.

There was a loud rumbling as Marius's mansion tottered. Branches pushed themselves out through the windows and roots broke through the walls, tearing them down. A corner of the mansion collapsed in a cloud of dust. Tiles rained down and shattered on the rubble.

The power of the Crocodile's Tear began to merge with that of the World's Egg. The two spiritstones were falling into harmony with each other. Tariq could sense Imix. Her thoughts and desires, her feelings of victory and defeat. The pride and the disappointment. She'd tried to fix it all, ignoring any alternatives. The other seers had looked to her for all the answers so she'd pretended, first to them, then to herself, that she had those answers. They'd trusted her too much. Her hubris had led them here.

She should have asked for help earlier. But she was asking for help now.

Tariq saw the animal spirits, like ghosts, standing beside the mortals, both the townsfolk and the pitiful hybrids. He saw Artos and Livia, the boar and the mouse. He needed to gently ease the person and the animal apart. He reached out with his own spirit, feeling Imix urging him on. She wanted him to learn, to pass on her knowledge of the Crocodile's Tear, and what better way than this? Could he separate the beast from the mortal?

Some resisted. Some liked the power, the abilities, that came with being animals. But deep down they knew it was wrong, unnatural.

One by one he saw the animal spirits fade, abandoning their mortal hosts.

Tariq slowly peeled open his eyes to see if the changes in the spirit world were being repeated here.

Artos squealed. He thrashed his tusked head from side to side, stamping his feet in anger, in pain. Livia was curled up in a ball, twitching uncontrollably.

The other animals were in equal torment. A flock of geese flapped and honked while a cow ran round in circles and a donkey bucked and brayed.

Alongside the ancient seer, Tariq continued to pour his power, his feelings, into the spiritstones.

Imix's eyes were half open and her lips slightly parted in a trance. The Crocodile's Tear shone brighter, beams of its light passing out between her fingers and striking all within range. Weird shadows twisted and writhed as the animals were pushed into a panicked frenzy.

The trees grew faster. They tore down buildings and their roots broke up the newly laid paving. The boughs swelled with fruit.

'Tariq?'

Artos stumbled towards him, checking his face anxiously. 'Do . . . do I still have tusks?' He was back to his usual self. Artos gazed at his hands, wiggling his fingers in amazement.

'She did it,' he murmured, almost as if he couldn't believe it.

Livia stretched, raising her arms as high as she could, bathing herself in the light of the new day. She was human again! Then she turned to them both and reached out. 'Hugs?'

Artos grunted. 'Oh, all right. Just this once.'

Back together again. Like it should be.

Tariq squeezed both friends against him. He wasn't going to let go of them, ever.

It wasn't Artos who broke the hug but Livia. She gazed at them, smiling even as tears filled her eyes. Tariq knew exactly how she felt as he wiped his cheeks.

Artos shifted from foot to foot, clearing his throat. 'Hugs aren't so bad, after all.'

All around them wandered townsfolk, some sobbing, others just dazed, all back to their original forms. One or two were still struggling out of their animal habits; one man continued flapping his arms like a bird.

'What about the hybrids?' asked Livia.

Tariq grinned as he pointed over towards an approaching crowd, with Foriz carried aloft on their shoulders.

The people howled, hooted and roared, mimicking the beasts they had once been but were no longer. By combining their power, Imix and Tariq had freed the hybrids from their tortured existence. The group cheered as they lowered Foriz to the ground. She was blushing as she approached them.

Artos shook his head. 'I'm never going to get used to that.'

'Used to what?' asked Livia.

'Foriz smiling,' he said, grinning himself.

Foriz looked at Tariq, her brow slightly furrowed. 'I didn't think you could do it. You're more powerful than I expected.'

He gestured towards Imix. 'She did most of it. I just helped a little.'

Foriz scowled as she looked over at the old seer.

'That makes no difference. She still needs to be punished for what she did.'

'I suppose. But not by me. I can't sit in judgement of another person.'

Imix was old, kept alive now by the power of the Crocodile's Tear she held limply in her bony, crooked fingers. 'Tariq?' The word hissed from her brittle chest. Each breath was a rattling gasp. She tilted her head back and forth as she smiled. 'Did it work?'

'Can't you . . .?'

She was blind. Time had caught up with her at last.

He knelt down in front of the ancient seer. 'Thank you.'

She sighed. 'What a team we could have made, Tariq. Your parents sang your praises from the moment they joined me. No parents could be prouder of their child. And when you arrived, I wondered what strange fate had given me such an opportunity, especially as you came with the World's Egg. It is time the spiritstones were reunited, and I thought, arrogantly, it was my destiny to gather them. But it's yours.'

Tariq shook his head. 'I'm only thirteen. What about my parents? The stones should stay here.'

'The spiritstones should stay with you, and Xibalba is not your home. Go and find the Heart's Desire, the third stone.'

'Where?'

'I gave it to one of my apprentices, Toril.'

'That's a korrish name.'

Imix nodded. 'She came from the north. That's where she will have taken it.'

North. It was a vast inhospitable land of mountains covered in snow for much of the year and dominated by small isolated kingdoms constantly at war with each other over the sparse resources. The people there were infamous for being tough, brutal.

Imix smiled. 'Ah, Sugreev.'

The silver gorilla loomed over them. It looked down at Tariq and growled softly.

Imix tutted. 'Hush now. Tariq did what he had to do. Come, my old friend, take me somewhere I can finally rest.'

The silver gorilla gently cradled Imix in its

arms and turned away. People parted in silence to let them go.

Dad came up to him, and put his arm over Tariq's shoulders as they watched. He sighed. 'So ends the age of legends.'

CHAPTER 33

ARTOS

Artos counted the ships on the horizon.

'Six. That should be enough for us all. Especially as we're travelling light. Thanks, Foriz.'

Foriz slapped his shoulder. 'Who'd have thought you'd be hiring smugglers to take you back to Ethrial.'

'Independent traders,' he replied, bristling. 'I've drawn up a contract to keep it all legal.'

'Whatever you want to call them, just as long as they get paid.'

A salty wind blew in off the sea. Seagulls cried out, eager for their breakfast. People were camped along the shore. No one wanted to reclaim New Ethrial. The seers of Xibalba mingled with the townsfolk – they'd brought food and shelter and helped them to deal with the time they'd been animals. One of the soldiers still barked when he got excited.

Artos faced Foriz. 'I'm surprised that you're not coming back with us. You sure? I could have a word with my father; he could make you a free woman with the stroke of his quill. You could start a new life back in Ethrial with a clean slate.'

'I've had enough of the big city. I want to try things here. The others feel the same. Plenty of the shipped have nothing to go back to. Now we've got our own town. That's a clean enough slate for us. We don't owe Ethrial anything.'

Artos gazed at the encroaching jungle suspiciously. So much of the town had been wrecked by the battle and, even two weeks later, there was still a huge amount of clearing needing to be done. 'It'll be a tough life.'

'To begin with,' said Foriz. 'Then it'll be great.'

There was a sudden rumble of an engine and a cheer. A plume of smoke rose over the trees.

Foriz smiled. 'Looks like Livia's got the Harvester fixed. I'd better go over and have her explain how it works.'

'A new life, then.' Artos held out his hand. 'Good luck, Foriz.'

They faced each other, the criminal and the Silver Guard. They'd been raised to hate each other but had found out they were more alike than different. They both fought for what they believed in. That was worth a friendship.

Foriz took his grip firmly. 'Goodbye, Artos.'

He watched her go, nodding to the others who'd decided to stay. Foriz had created a criminal empire out of nothing back home, and if anyone could make this town work, it was her. He just hoped—

'Put those down there. Be gentle! That's the china!'

Artos groaned even as he turned towards the commotion on the one remaining quay.

Lord Marius had claimed it as his. He was

governor, after all. His servants were stacking crates while Marius, bedecked in his finest and wearing a hat with three peacock plumes, directed them.

'And that goes alongside the crate with the curtains. Be careful! Those are worth more than your entire year's salary!' He waved his hat frantically at the exhausted servant. 'Oh, why are you so useless!? The moment I get back to Ethrial you're all fired!'

Artos climbed up the ladder from the beach. 'Problems, sir?'

Marius shoved his hat back on. 'Nothing that concerns you, guardsman.'

'There's no room for those crates. We've a lot of people to get home.'

Marius gazed down at the crowd. 'They can live in the hold for all I care. That's how half of them got here anyway. I am not leaving without my belongings.'

'Then you're more than welcome to stay.'

Lord Marius glared at him. 'I will have words with your father when I get home. I promise you that.'

'You do that.' Artos rested his foot on one of the crates. 'What's in here?'

'A hundred-piece dining set. The goblets are all crystal. You have to treat it with—'

Artos shoved it into the sea.

'What are you doing?!' screamed Marius.

Artos summoned the servants. 'Throw it *all* into the sea.'

CHAPTER 34
LIVIA

Livia released the brake. The Harvester shook, as if loosening its limbs for a day's work, and took its first step. Its front feet sank into the mud, then settled and began plodding.

The crowd cheered and Livia grinned.

All her exhaustion just lifted. The two weeks of hammering, forging, fixing and rebuilding had all been worth it. She'd fixed it! More than fixed it, she'd made it better than ever.

She spotted Foriz emerge from the trees and Livia waved at her. 'Come up here!'

Foriz sprinted alongside and then with a nimble spring leapt up beside her, hanging off the engine while Livia steered.

Foriz passed her gaze over the machine. 'It looks so different now.'

Livia's grin broadened. 'Amazing, isn't it? All redesigned within a fortnight!'

'You're a true engineer. I wouldn't even know where to start.'

Livia blushed. A true engineer. That was what she wanted to be more than anything. She cleared her throat as she steadied the wheel. They were coming up to the edge of the field; they'd need to turn round soon. 'Want me to explain how it all works?'

Foriz arched an eyebrow. 'Unless you want to stay too? There's plenty for you here, Livia. I've seen your sketchbooks, all those plants, insects and creatures you've drawn. There's a whole world waiting to be discovered.'

Livia wanted to, so badly, but she shook her

head. 'One day perhaps. But we came here to find the Crocodile's Tear. Time to go elsewhere.'

'For the third spiritstone? The Heart's Desire?' asked Foriz.

'The quest isn't over.' Livia turned the wheel slowly. The Harvester made a wide arc at the edge of the field and began heading back the way it had come. 'You need to treat the machine gently. It may look like a great big monster but it's your friend. The engine's simple. Just keep it fuelled with wood and clean it out after every job. Make sure you don't leave any ash to clog up the exhausts. And the blades . . .' She looked over her shoulder at the new arrangement. 'File down any damage they might have from stones, and oil them once a month. They'll last a lifetime. I guarantee it.'

The claws were gone. They'd not be needed now. She'd taken the six blades and, with the help of the local blacksmith, reforged them into ploughs. Three plough blades working simultaneously. The Harvester could plough a big field in a morning. If she'd had more time, she would have invented a device to sprinkle the seeds, but there were farmers amongst the shipped who knew the business of growing better than her.

'In this soil you'd get two yields a year. More than enough for the town, with plenty to store or sell.'

Livia pulled the brake. 'Try it.'

Foriz stared at her. 'What if I run someone over?'

'Just . . . don't? Halfway across the field start turning it round slowly. By the time you get to the end you'll be facing the way you came.'

The crowd gave a huge cheer as Foriz took the controls. Livia clambered off and made sure she was far out of the way. 'Release the brake and remember . . . gently does it!'

The machine juddered, but then, with a few initial faltering steps, it began plodding on, and Livia watched the blades – ploughs – churn up the soil behind, ready for whatever crops needed planting.

Foriz sat up in the seat, beaming with joy.

Livia stood and watched. She was covered in mud and soot. Her clothes were singed by embers from the forge and her hands covered in blisters and cuts, but she'd never felt more herself. She'd done the redesign on scraps of paper, calculations counting with pebbles from the beach and *made it work*.

Like a true engineer.

CHAPTER 35
TARIQ

How could he say goodbye to his parents? He'd only just found them. The last two weeks had been the best: exploring the jungle, shape-changing back and forth from eel, learning from the other seers. But now the ships had come, just as Foriz had promised.

Mum and Dad stood with him on the beach. Those who were heading back had already boarded and the ships were waiting to weigh anchor. Tariq had found every excuse to delay leaving but there were no excuses left.

Dad put a sack of fruit on the sand. 'Make sure you eat well. I know what ship food can be like.'

'Yes, Dad.'

Mum straightened his new tunic and ran her fingers through his hair. She sniffed. 'Send Nani our love.'

'Yes, Mum.'

'We'll see each other again,' she said, tears in her eyes.

'Yes, Mum.' Tariq blinked, the tears almost blinding him. 'I don't want to go.'

She hugged him. He didn't care if she crushed him; he didn't want to leave the embrace, ever.

'Your friends are coming,' said Dad, his voice gruff. He wiped his wet cheeks. 'You're my brave boy. Do you know that? A hero.'

'I don't feel brave. Why don't you come with me?'

They looked at each other. Dad smiled as he cupped Tariq's face. 'We discussed this. Your friends need you. Our people need us, especially now Imix is gone.'

Tariq nodded sadly. 'But you'll be so far away. I don't want to lose you again.'

Mum kissed his forehead. 'You'll never lose us.'

He nodded, too full of feeling to speak. He broke away reluctantly, and Dad gripped his shoulders as he inspected him. 'Follow your heart, Tariq. It won't lead you astray.'

His parents retreated to the top of the beach, along with those from the town who'd decided to stay, the shipped and the seers from Xibalba. Quite a crowd had gathered to see the three of them off.

Artos patted Tariq on the shoulder and Livia squeezed his hand, smiling sympathetically.

If his friends needed him, then he needed them *more*.

Tariq pointed towards the sea. 'Time to go home.'

They'd gathered their belongings. Livia had her various tool kits neatly stacked on the sand while Artos had buckled on his armour, the steel polished like a mirror. He was sweating and the sun wasn't even halfway up, but he was a Silver Guard, even if his scabbard was empty.

'What if we get attacked by pirates? What will you fight with?' Tariq asked.

'Anything I can get my hands on. And if there's nothing nearby . . .' he lifted his fists, '. . . these will do.'

Tariq nodded. 'Fair enough.'

Artos smiled. 'It'll be autumn by the time we're back in Ethrial. It's beautiful then. All the trees are covered in gold; the air's fresher too. I cannot wait to get my feet back on cobblestones, where they belong.'

'I'm not lingering in Ethrial.' Tariq patted his satchel, heavier now it held two spiritstones. 'I'm going after the Heart's Desire.'

After what had happened here, realising what power was available through the use of the spiritstones, he felt a new urgency to find the third and last of them. Was it like the World's Egg, hidden away somewhere all but forgotten? Or was someone using it even now? And if so, were they using it wisely or for their own ambition?

'You're keeping both the spiritstones now?' asked Artos.

Tariq frowned. 'I offered to leave the Crocodile's Tear at Xibalba, but my parents and the other seers thought the two spiritstones should be kept together for now. Once I find the third, who knows. Bring them back here perhaps.'

'You've gone up in the world, Tariq. I remember when we first met – your first day in Ethrial and already in a whole heap of trouble.'

Tariq smiled. 'It's good I've got you to keep me out of it!'

Artos looked at him. 'So where we will find the Heart's Desire?'

'We?' asked Tariq. 'What about the cobblestones of Ethrial?'

'Where you go, I go,' said Artos gruffly. 'Who else will keep you out of trouble?'

Tariq laughed. 'Maybe our troubles are behind us! One tidal wave, one animal invasion. We deserve a break, don't you think?'

Livia gazed out at the approaching rowboat, the last. 'I do, but somehow I don't think we'll be getting one.'

Tariq fell silent. His eyes looked brighter now,

or maybe it was just the morning sun. The river boy was transforming into a powerful seer. Who knew what was ahead for any of them.

Tariq suddenly held out his hand. 'Thanks, both of you.'

Artos laid his on top and Livia did the same on top of his. 'Together, no matter what,' she said.

Tariq nodded. 'No matter what.'

Livia rubbed her glasses. 'So if we're not staying in Ethrial, where are we headed?'

'North. Imix told me that was where the third stone was taken.'

Artos winced. 'The old kingdoms? That's going to be tough. The northern korrs don't like outsiders. They're . . . traditional. Not like us city folk. Not so much into making deals round a table, more into solving their conflicts with axes.'

'Nothing the three of us can't handle, eh?' said Tariq.

The rowboat was hauled up on to the beach and the captain, a smuggler ally of Foriz's, waved to them.

Artos grimaced. 'Sailing home with smugglers. I hope my father doesn't find out.'

Livia clapped him on the shoulder. 'Just wait till we're in sight of Ethrial before you decide to arrest them all.'

They helped haul their belongings on to the boat. Artos managed to clamber on board, even in his armour, while Livia directed the rowers as they loaded up her tool kits. The captain held out his hand and pulled Tariq out of the surf and on to the boat.

'Where are all your belongings?' he asked.

Tariq patted his satchel. 'Right here.'

Crates bobbed in the water nearby. One had broken open and a carpet had been washed up. It was from Kilim, very expensive. Tariq hoped the crabs would appreciate it.

'I still have family in the mountains,' said Artos. 'It's about time I visited them. They'll look after us while we search for the Heart's Desire.'

'Do you know much about the third spiritstone?' asked Livia.

Artos shrugged. 'The clue's in the name, don't you think?'

'That makes me worry. You can't let anyone know you're searching for it, Tariq. Most people believe the spiritstones are just legends, the stuff of fairy tales. Now word's spreading they're real, others will be keen to get their hands on them.'

'Come on, lads! Ain't you in a hurry to get home?' said the captain from the prow. 'Put your backs into it!'

Each stroke took them further away from the shore. The crowd began to disperse; they had work to do and it was a long way back to Xibalba. Not his parents, though. They stayed, waving. They wanted to see them all the way over the horizon.

The ship loomed ahead. It was a sleek sailing ship designed for speed and discretion. It would get them back to Ethrial in half the time it had taken getting here. A sailor tossed down a rope ladder and the captain grabbed it as the rowboat was buffeted alongside. He pointed at Artos. 'You first.'

It wasn't easy but Artos managed to get from one end of the rowboat to the other without falling over. He took hold of the rope ladder, gulped as he gazed at the deep water, and began climbing. The rowers cheered as he made it on deck. Livia followed even as the rowers began loading her tool kits into a net that dangled over the side of the hull.

Then Tariq climbed up. A sailor grabbed his hand to help him on to the deck. The rest of the crew were busy getting ready to leave. The five other ships were already heading for the horizon.

'Get that anchor up!' yelled the captain, the moment he was onboard.

Seagulls circled overhead. The air was thick with salt and the promise of adventure.

They had two of the spiritstones. Tariq had witnessed the power of the World's Egg and the Crocodile's Tear, world-changing magic that was beyond understanding. And now they were after the final stone, the Heart's Desire. Getting it wouldn't be easy. He'd come close to death countless times getting the first two – what would be the cost they'd have to pay to get the third?

They'd find out soon enough.

TO BE CONCLUDED . . .

NEW YORK TIMES BESTSELLING AUTHOR
SARWAT CHADDA

Sarwat Chadda was an engineer for twenty years, before taking the leap into the world of writing. His novels for children have been published in many countries and have appeared on the *New York Times* Bestseller list. Sarwat loves to write about fantasy and high adventure, mixing myths and legends into the real world. A keen traveller, Sarwat has visited many different countries, which often inspires his work. When he's not writing or travelling the world, Sarwat loves playing tabletop games and is a Dungeons and Dragons game master. Sarwat lives in London with his wife and attention-grabbing cat.

Feel free to contact him on X @sarwatchadda, on Instagram @sarwat_chadda, or at sarwatchadda.com.

COMING SOON!
The thrilling conclusion to

THE SPIRITSTONE SAGA

Have you read the first story in

THE SPIRITSTONE SAGA?

See where it all began in . . .

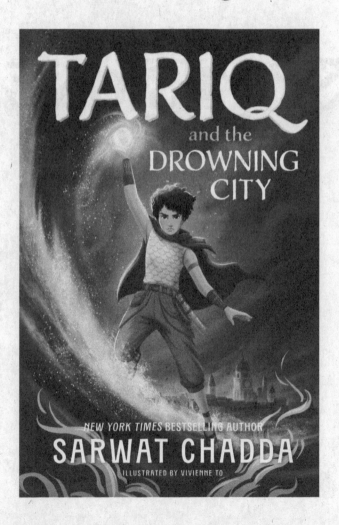

CHAPTER 1
TARIQ

Everyone froze when the bell started ringing. It clanged from the great bell tower, its heavy toll echoing across the city. Its citizens stared at each other, bewildered. Then the ground shook, tiles fell from the roofs and the trees swayed. The canals through the city flooded, washing the narrow streets and wide piazzas with greenish, befouled water.

People ran for the gates, knocking over market stalls, tripping and trampling over those slower, weaker than themselves. They fought each other as they tried to cross the bridges spanning the canals – some wide, most not – pushing, shoving, not caring who was thrown over into the now broiling waters, not looking back to people begging for help as they sank, still clinging to whatever meagre belongings mattered to them most.

Tariq watched it all from the top of the bell tower. He let go of the bell rope and faced the sea.

The wave rose higher and higher. A few ships hadn't made it to harbour before the immense sea gates had closed. The wave smashed them to splinters and dragged the remains down into the deep.

But one boat battled on.

It was silver and small, and rode the waves with stubborn determination, galloping over the huge crests. The sea raged against it, and yet the tiny silver craft fought on, the last hope of an entire city.

Then the tidal wave struck the walls, the bell tower crumbled as if made of sand. Tariq fell, fell into the swirling, roaring, fathomless depths . . .

*

'Tariq? What's wrong? Tariq?'

Tariq gasped, flailing as if he was still tumbling. He stared around frantically, bewildered at what was real and what was a dream, until he saw Nani squatting beside him.

She was real. She always was.

She put her hand against his forehead. 'You're hot. You got a fever?'

'I'm fine. Really. It was just . . . nothing,' he lied, quickly throwing off his blanket and getting up. The rest of the clan were already packed, with rafts loaded and canoes being pushed off the bank into the water. 'We have to pack. We can't keep everyone waiting.'

Nani wanted to ask more, but instead turned towards the dawn sun. 'We've got a long way ahead of us, but by tonight we'll be in our new home. Our home in Ethrial.' She lumbered to the canoe with her bedding, but suddenly doubled over as she started coughing.

'Just need a sip of water. *Clean* water.'

Tariq knew what she meant. Once, they'd merely dip their hands in the river and scoop out a mouthful, watching the droplets sparkle through their fingers. Not now. Not since the business owners of Ethrial had lined the rivers with factories and diverted the streams that the clan had lived off for countless generations. Not since the building of the Four Rivers Dam.

If you drank from the river now, you got sick. The fish had found new streams to swim in. The animals that had once thrived on these familiar banks had perished. The river stank of rot.

Read TARIQ AND THE DROWNING CITY
to find out what happens next!